I0563907

The Mole Hunters Children

Alex Mitchell

Published by Alex Mitchell, 2024.

This is a work of fiction. Similarities to real people, places, or events are entirely coincidental.

THE MOLE HUNTERS CHILDREN

First edition. January 29, 2024.

Copyright © 2024 Alex Mitchell.

ISBN: 979-8891980259

Written by Alex Mitchell.

.

Also by Alex Mitchell

Welcome to Shepherds Pass
Revenge at Shepherds Pass
Treasure at Shepherds Pass
Welcome to Shepherds Pass
Man Among the Missing
Noreen Tyler
Robinhood at Shepherds Pass
That Which Makes Us Who We Are
Secrets That Bind Family
Balance of Power in Shepherds Pass
All Gods Children
The Mole Hunters Children

I dedicate this book to Dorothy (Blondie), Joyce, Patricia, Barbara* and Annette my sisters and to Robert P, Dale*, Carl, and Ched my brothers. I also dedicate this book to the gaggle of children, grandchildren, great grandchildren, niece, and nephews what we have and will produce. Families are a living thing and therefore must grow to survive.

The Mold Hunters Children

Chapter one

"What's the new book about?" Bonnie Asked. Detective Victoria "Bonnie" Blake and Detective John D Spencer sat rushing down Highway 70 to answer a call.

They are members of the St. Louis Major Case Squad. The St. Louis Major Case Squad is comprised of Seasoned Detectives who have been incorporated from various departments to solve the most heinous or complex crimes.

These detectives usually have at least five years in law enforcement with at least two years as an investigator.

Unlike most squads, they assist local law agencies and cover the Missouri Counties of St. Louis, St. Charles, Jefferson, Warren, and Lincoln. They also are involved in operations in Madison, St. Clair, Monroe, Jersey, Macoupin, Bond, Clinton, and Randolph Counties in Illinois.

"It's not a novel, Detective," Spencer answered, keeping his eyes on the traffic as he drove.

The Major Case Squad has a unique structure in that it can allow an individual Detective or pair of Detective to work on a case, or it can, as is often the cases, enable many Detectives to be brought into a case, therefore allowing a variety of specialties and experiences to be put to bare on an issue.

"It still has to be about something, don't it?"

Bonnie's Alabama twang command as she searched the onboard computer for information on the occupants of the home they were driving to.

Spencer pretended to be slightly annoyed with her query, but he was sure she saw through it. He enjoyed the professional aspects of their relationship. He was also aware that she barely qualified for the squad due to her young age and barely meeting the investigation minimum requirement. Still, she looked to him as something of a mentor.

"It's a textbook. The way it works with most textbooks is that there is a group of different subjects. Various Authors write them then the material is edited to cover the required subject matter."

"So, what is the subject matter you are writing about?"

"It is a comparative analysis of community policing now compared to what has been done in past decades and the need for evolution of techniques and strategies as the police evolve."

"Quite a mouth full."

"The text will replace some outdated training material in use."

AS THEY EXITED THE Highway, they could see a shift in traffic. This was not good, in that this far from the crime scene was concerned, a traffic slow down meant that many vehicles were on the scene and some traffic had been diverted. In the St. Louis Metro area, many of the neighborhoods are residential. Which means many of the main streets branch out to residential streets. Many of the residential streets are turn-around or cul de sacs with no outlets to through traffic.

"Utilities is listed to Patrick L. Boone—age 52. Semi-retired, as far as I can see. No Mrs. Boone listed—three young children. No arrest. No warrants. Several firearms in his name." Detective Blake reported.

"Any idea what he is semi-retired from?"

"No clue here."

"I like flying blind as much as the next guy, but I hope someone on the scene asks the right questions."

As the unmarked police car dove approaching the address listed as the scene, it was nothing short of spectacular. There was an undetermined number of police cars, all with their lights flashing. As it was early evening in the fall, the sun had already gone down, and the darker it got, the more dominant the unsynchronized flashing of lights created a surreal, hypnotic effect. There was a large number of ambulances and emergency vehicles of an undetermined origin. There were so many vehicles responding that some were parked on the lawns of homes in the cul de sac. There was a large group of houses making up the neighborhood; all had a similar building style. Leading to the impression that they had all been built about the same time; however, the owners had resisted being clones and had done various additions and remolding projects to assert their individuality. All the houses seem to have uniformed officers in pairs or threesomes interviewing the residents. Teams of officers walked converging in the narrow street. As they spotted the house, they assumed it was the point of concern. They had to slow down, knowing they would not be able to park close to the home. As they drove slowly, a tall black police officer in a crisp City police uniform with a white shirt walked up to the car. It was Sargent JD Robinson. Spencer knew Robinson from previous cases and had a great respect for him. Robinson was a natural-born leader, and offices followed him out of respect with little second-guessing his choices or commands.

Robinson had been involved in college football and still looked like he could take the field on any given Sunday.

"How bad is it, JD?" Spencer asked, rolling down the car windows.

"Well, boss, anytime the police call the police, it aint good. It's Slater's party, and I think he will kiss both of you when he sees you."

Robinson smiled completely and motioned for them to park and walk the rest of the way to the house. Spencer squeezed the car behind a poorly parked Toyota and what looked like a CSI unit with the back doors open and a wide array of impossible-to-identify tools in the back.

"So, Sargent Slater is there, and he doesn't like me. I am only telling you because you are my partner, and I would never let you get blindsided."

Detective Blake offered lightly, grabbing Spencer's arm as he started to exit the car.

"Is there a reason why?"

Yes, but it is personal.

"Excepted. Then you don't have to tell me."

"But what if I want to."

"Blake...." He stared before she interrupted.

"You promised to call me Bonnie when we are not around other people." Bonnie's homey twain again ran through.

"Sorry, I must have lost my head." He grinned. "Look, if it is something personal, there is an army of female Cop and Counselors who would give their right arm to hear whatever it is that is personal."

Robinson began staring at the two detectives seated in the car with a look that seemed to read. Gee, I hope they did not decide to back out of this mess.

"Look. I know I am not as smart as you. And I know people are always trying to pick your brain, then take whatever they learn and try to palm it off as their own. But that's not me. Aside from being your partner in the chicken-picking town, you are the closest thing I have to a friend. She averted his gaze as if slightly embarrassed by something she had memorized and meant to tell him but now had to think about how it sounded.

"Blake, sorry, Bonnie, I will be happy to listen to whatever the problem between you and Slater. I know he is a good guy, but if he is giving you Shit."

"No. You see, the problem is when I first got here, I went out with his son a couple of times."

God, this is personal, Spencer thought to himself. What did I agree to?

"His son is a Cop."

"Yes, I know Kyle." Spencer clarified.

"I tried to get him in bed."

"Are you sure you wouldn't rather be talking to a female?"

"No. Because his son confessed to me that he wanted to date me to throw his father off the track. Kyle is Gay."

"Oh." Which was all Spencer could muster as a retort. Suddenly, the mayhem that was inside the house ahead seemed a lot more promising than this conversation.

"I don't know how you all St. Louis people plan your lives, but I want a house full of kids someday. I am from a family of Fourteen, and well, maybe not that many for myself, but how many can I get from a man I got to worry about who, when he says he is out shaking it with the boys, might really be out shaking it with the boys if you know what I mean?" She stopped and looked at Spencer as if wisdom would spout from his lips.

"Detective." He began, and she looked at him with an eye of correction. "Bonnie, no one is worth being trapped in a marriage without real love or hope. You say you want children. No mother in her right mind would knowingly commit her children to a life of endless pain and mental hell." He stared off a bit as if remembering events from his past.

"Oh, damn, I screwed up. I never meant to drop my pain off on you and have you relive it ten times over." She was not sure what the reflection in his past called to mind. She patted his arm to let him know she appreciated his consul.

"Let's say we go round up some bad guys. That always makes us feel better."

"DICK. BIG DICK, OVER here." A young woman shouted to Detective Spencer as the two detectives attempted to approach Sargent Slater. The young woman was Morgan Boone, the homeowner's daughter they would soon meet. She wore a tight, long-sleeved running shirt and running pants in a neon color. Her dark hair was restrained as if she had just come from a workout or run. She had been stopped from entering the house and stood in the company of four uniformed officers who circled her. As she shouted, many neighbors answering questions for officers or assessing broken window damage on their property stopped to hear what was being said. News vans and camera crews were slogging up the incline leading to the house.

"Hey, Big Dick, don't ignore me."

"Is there something you want to share with me, my dear Detective Spencer?" Detective Blake asked in her most southern twang while batting her eye lashes.

"Hold that thought." He responded, walking to the young woman. Slater joined Blake and waited for the outcome of the confrontation.

Slater did not look or address Blake directly, and she knew this as a shuttle snub, but she had endured worse. It was snubs or insults that were not of her accounting for that troubled her.

Detective Spencer was a little over six feet. He was lean and muscular and showed no outward signs of frailty. He leaned on the patrol car where the young woman was being corralled with his back to the car and rested. She rested beside him, eyeing him from head to toe.

"Have we met?" He asked.

"No. I'm Morgan Boone. I live here. These clowns say I can't go into my own house. They say they are waiting for the leader. I say that would be the ringmaster." She paused and smiled. "They say no, it would be the Dick in charge."

"So, you are assuming that makes me the big dick?"

She looked at him and assumed she had made her point.

"Please let me make a couple of things clear to help us both. First, I have been here less than ten minutes, and I don't even know if this is a case I will be taking over." He spoke in a clear, modulated tone, then turned to face her. "Look around. You said it yourself: this is a circus and getting worse by the minute. Please. Please give me a little time to figure out where I am and what is happening."

Her look at him softened as she waited for him to continue.

"I promise if I am taking this case, I will talk to you, and I will do so as respectfully as I can, even if you choose to do the opposite." Her soft brown eyes now had the deer trapped in a headlight look he was going for.

He smiled ever so slightly and leaned close to her to whisper so the police watching them could not hear. "You see all these ugly old women in ugly in old ugly house coats. Please stop referring to me as Big Dick because I don't want them following me home."

"Morgan giggled." Morgan Boone is nineteen, an age where woman and girl thoughts collide in most young females. Still, there was something else in the exchange that made her need to jockey for control of the encounter. She had a slender frame accentuated with large breasts that had the stand-at-attention quality that women frequently spent their later years trying to imitate or reconstruct, but for her. for here and now, the wonders of the young stood proudly. Something about this man, she thought he was good in his heart. What's more, harassing him would have its limits. "The sun has gone down, and it is getting cold out here." She announced.

Spencer removed his police windbreaker and wrapped it around Morgan. He gently rubbed her arms. "That should be a little better. And please stop harassing my guys." Spencer could feel Blake staring into the back of his head.

He knew she was wondering if this was part of the lessons she was supposed to learn. They had been together only about six months, and she felt she learned more from him in six months than in all the time spent anywhere in her life. Also, a pang of jealousy echoed in her. She was not quite sure why it was there or what course it was taking, but it was there.

"Yeah, Spencer, is that good stuff just for the teeny boppers, or can a middle-aged girl put in a bid?" A female officer called out as Slater began leading Spencer and Blake to the first item, he was waiting to show them. This brought a hearty round of laughter and jeers from many of the officers and some of the otherwise stoic news crew. Slater held a large envelope in his hand but did not refer to it directly.

"Tonight's bill of fare starts with hors d'oeuvre. Please let me assist you with the menu." Sargent Slater began. "Nice of you to join us, Spencer. It feels like old times." Sargent bellowed. Sargent Raymond Slater was a police sergeant of distinction. He was tall in his early sixties in calendar age but had a strong, tall, youthful body. His posture was perfect, and he looked like a football coach who could take the field and outdo even his best starters to prove a point. Slater had been in many ranks in his career but currently had been put back as Sargent. He had issues with authority. He did not like it when politics interfered with the operation of his job and did not back down. The quality, while making him circumspect with his superior, endeared him to the men and women under his supervision. Even more to the point, he was a supervisor's supervisor. Other supervisors came to him for answers, not only on a tactical or procedural quandary but also on difficult-to-deal-with personnel issues.

Slater had joined Detectives Spencer and Blake as they walked up the hill toward the house that was the main center of attention. He had ignored Blake's presence altogether. An apparent snub that she was still willing to ignore outwardly.

"Which old times, Ray, you are thinking, Pruitt-Igoe Projects or Downtown East St. Louis?"

"I'm thinking more downtown Beirut in the spring," Slater responded.

As Blake was walking up the grass, where there was a group of men standing in a circle on the neighboring lawn, she slipped and lost her footing.

In a flash, Slater caught her arm, preventing her from falling. "Sorry, Detective, my fault. I should have mentioned it is all slippery of the grass due to a lot of early morning dew.

Blake corrected her step and gave a slight glance to Spencer. Surely, this was something they would need to review later.

The group parted as Blake and Spencer reached them.

"This is your idea of a hors d'oeuvre?" Blake asked.

On the ground was a man in full tactical body gear lying face down in the mud. There were rips in the legs of his pants, showing huge holes where he had been shot.

There was blood covering much in his lower uniform, and blood from a separated source covered the upper portion.

"Test." Spencer announced, looking at Blake, "What do we see?"

She removed a pen and a small pad from her jacket pocket and began to scribble. She also seemed to be drawing small pictures.

"This guy was shot over at the house where we are going. He made it over the four-foot fence between the properties. Another man was helping him. "She pointed at the ground. "The second man has feet like sasquatch—two sets of footprints. The dearly departed is about a size nine to nine and a half. The most common men's shoe size in the world, I might add." She turned toward the ground near where she had lost her footing. It seemed clear to the men that she was distracted by something she saw in the mud. "A truck pulled up there. Probably a dually or heavy-duty model. Something with an extra wide wheelbase. You know that because only one wheel hit the mud, the other tire was outside where most wheelbase ranges are. Our departed was hurt bad. I suspect that the ME will tell you the shots to the leg hit the femoral artery."

"Shouldn't there have been more blood loss for that type of wound?" One of the men who had made the circle asked as if that was a significant part of what was being discussed before she started her recitation.

"Normally, Yes, but there is enough space in the thigh for an internal bleed of critical proportion."

She looked at Spencer before continuing.

He nodded for her to continue. "If I may speculate, the big buy told the little guy if you can walk to the vehicle on your own, you are a go to go. The minute the little guy fell to the ground, showing he was not going to make it, the big guy pulled out his sidearm and shot his friend in the head." She lifted the helmet the little guy was wearing, and it exposed a bullet wound to the temple. "And we know his friend shot him because even if he could drag himself twenty-five feet and crawl over a four-foot fence while bleeding to death. He could not make it out of this spot with a 45 in his brain, and there are burn marks and stippling suggesting contact with the head at the time of discharge." She stopped looking down at the notes she had been busy scribbling and looked at Spencer for approval.

Slater looked at her with a look of amazement. "Spencer, you want to add anything."

"In just a moment." Spencer smiled.

"Well, that being the case, tonight's menu comes with soup, salad, and breadsticks," Slater offered, and he began to lead the troop toward the exterior of the Boone house.

Spencer could see Morgan watching him, waiting with an interested look.

"Guys, it's Spencer." A short, chubby man called through the hole that used to be a window.

"See, guys, he has a female partner. You own me Ten bucks."

"Your soup Detectives."

Slater pointed to a window that had been blasted out. The blast had also caused several neighboring homes to lose widows, and the angry homeowners stood nearby inspecting their properties. Through the missing window, you could see a large group of men and women taking samples and pictures. Many seemed preoccupied by something on the floor, but it was not viewable from the exterior where the Detectives stood. "Next up, salad." Slater continued his dinner at the crime scene theme. Blake thought it was a little cruel but kept writing.

Slater walked to a second window.

This one was in the backyard of the house. It has also been blasted out.

"This had to make noise to beat the band." Blake observed.

"One loud blast, then World War Three broke out. No one could count the shots." Slater commented. He led them to another perfectly intact window. "What room is this? Spencer asked.

"Good questions, Detective Spencer. Good to see you are paying attention. This is one of the bathrooms." They knew which rooms they wanted to enter through, so they had not only a game plan but also a floor plan. Blake kept scribbling furiously upon the revelations.

"And here we have our breadsticks." A third window was blown out at the South end of the house.

"Three blasts so close together they sound like one. Then, an entry team in tactical gear. Are you sure you didn't mean to call the army?" Spencer asked.

"Old friend, we haven't even reached the reason I called you. Shall we proceed to the entrée?"

"Is it my imagination, but are there guys hoping they don't have anything to do with whatever is happening here?" Blake whispered to Spencer as they walked toward the steps being led by Slater.

Spencer could not only detect the increased interest in Morgan's eyes as she watched the small group preparing to enter the house, but he could see changes in her face. Most police learn to be good at reading changes if facial tells, but this was a transformation; the out-of-control teen she had offered to distract him was now changing to something he could not discern as he approached the doorway to the house. Was it her relationship with the deceased, or maybe how he, the dead, came to be in such a state?

"And now, folks, the entrée." Slater offered.

Entering the house amazed the detectives. There were three bodies, all lying in pools of their own blood.

There was broken glass everywhere.

Hole patterns from automatic weapons fine was in every direction. Feathers from the stuffing of pillows that once filled the furniture lay resting on a sofa after obviously having floated through the onslaught. Solemness covered the room as did blood splatter. There was evidence of a terminal battle on every wall and even quite a bit on the ceiling.

Two of the men were dressed in the same tactical outfits as the small man lying dead in the yard. The third man lies face down in a robe.

"Hey, are we at war?"

One of the technical in lab coat and booties asked. "Don't read much, so if we have been invaded, this is the first I have heard of it." It was now clear to the detectives where the war references originated. There were always six technicians of one sort or other, but the men kept coming and going from the crime scene. There was also a half dozen uniform officers who were taking pictures and measuring thing.

The uniformed officers were busy going through doors and looking behind things.

"Femoral shots on this one. It looks like someone knew how to stop body-armored home invaders." Blake points to one of the bodies.

Spencer walked to the other body in armor and kneeled. "You guys find the knife?"

One of the uniformed officers, Officer Davis, looked at him confused.

"Keep your eyes on the ball, young man. Even with all the gunfire going on in this room, the guy was stabbed." He rolled the body slightly over. "Big blade killing knife. Upward right through the floating rib, through the lung, and into the heart. Judging from the color of the massive blood loss.

Even if this guy had been standing in the hospital with a team of surgeons on hand, he wouldn't have had a chance."

"No knife that I can see that matches what you are describing. The set in the kitchen is clean and in the holders." Slater answered.

Detective Boone stood and walked back to the body of the man in the robe. He had been a good-looking black man of medium pigment, not unlike the coloring of a Spanish, Cuban, or Mexican. It was clear now that the young girl outside was of mixed parenting. She had been blessed with the better features of both races.

The dead man's eyes were closed. Spencer suspected that if he opened them, they would reveal the same hazel brown that Morgan had displayed. His body was riddled with so many gunshots it was impossible on first inspection to tell the entrance wounds from the exit wounds.

Not that it mattered to the deceased. "Why is God's name....." Spencer muttered.

"We asked for God. They sent us you instead. Now I am out ten bucks. "One of the techs responded.

"Maybe she's a ringer. Are you a ringer, young lady?" Another tech directed toward Blake.

"What's a ringer?"

Blake asked, and this was due to a round of smiles from most of the people in the room.

"May I introduce you to the homeowner, the late Patrick L. Boone." Slater pointed to the man lying face down in the robe. The man had been shot multiple times. "Machine gunned from various directions; I always say if you are going to do a thing, do it right. The home had an open layout. The living room leads directly into the dining room. The body that had been shot in the thighs lay there face down near one of the windows that had been destroyed. It could not clearly be told from the first inspection whether the man had been coming or going when his life expired. The body with the knife wound to the heart lay in the kitchen, which was off the dining area near the kitchen cabinets, sink, dishwasher, stove, and refrigeration. All the cabinets except one were open.

A uniformed officer, Miller stood attempting to open the cabinet that would not budge. "Hey, Sarg, this one is stuck." No sooner than the patrolman had finished his assessment, the cabinet above the stove popped open, and the door hit the officer in the face, causing his nose to bleed. He was slightly disoriented when two little feet kicked him in the face, and a small girl jumped out of the cabinet. She was covered in blood and had a wild stare in her eyes. She also was carrying the missing knife, a plastic composite Randel combat knife. She swung the blade as the patrolman tried to grab her and cut a large gash across his hand. She pushed him out of the way just enough to spring from the top of the stove to the glass-covered floor. Her tiny feet immediately started bleeding. Wild-eyed, she stared at the people in the room. Another officer reached for her and grabbed her arm. She cut him across the thigh, and he screamed and let go. The little girl looked at the group of people now surrounding her and then over to the body of Patrick Boone, her father, as the body lay riddled with death. "Papa." She cried out. She backed toward the body as if to protect it, never minding that the shattered glass was marring her little feet. One of the officers drew his taser and pointed at the little girl.

Just as he was pulling the trigger, Detective Blake knocked his hands forward, and the projectiles released into the air toward the ceiling.

"Boy, are you out of your rabid-ass mind? I am not about to stand here and let you electrocute that baby." Sensing conflict, the little girl's eye took on a puzzled look. "Papa."

She cried through her tears.

Blake dropped to her knees and opened her arms toward the child. The knees of Blake's jeans rested in the mirid of broken glass, and it was unclear to anyone, even herself, if or how much she was being cut. "What kind of moron are you?" Blake spat at the patrolman.

"Papa gone, baby, and I think you need to cry for him. Come here, and I will hold and protect you, and we will cry for Papa."

The little girl looked at Blake and, for a second, pointed the knife at her. "Baby, I am here on my knees, and I can't run from you or to you. But I know you need to cry for Papa. Now you don't need that big old knife. You see that guy over there."

Blake directed her look to Spencer. "He is maybe my best friend in the whole wide world, and if you give him that knife, I promise if you and I need that knife, he will give it right back to us."

Amber Boone thought for a moment, then started giving the knife to Spencer. Amber made sure to hand the butt side of the knife to Spencer, and it was obvious that it registered that she had been trained on the correct way to pass a knife.

He wore disposable gloves, produced a plastic bag from his pocket, and deposited the knife. Almost as if a single bound, Amber leaped to Blake and hugged her. Blake sat gently, rocking the child.

"Get Child services in here." Spencer requested no one in particular, and one of the officers ran out of the room.

Blake held up the one finger, showing she needed a little time as the child cried.

"Can we send him off?" Blake asked the child, Amber.

Amber nodded in the affirmative. Blake held Amber tightly. "Our Father Who are in heaven," Blake began, and Amber joined her. "Howarth be thy name." as the remaining techs and officers joined in the Lord's Prayer. At the amen, it was clear that everyone in the room had joined in a choir to send Patrick L Boone off to wherever his soul was destined. Amber looked a little less like a wild child. She leaned forward and whispered into Blake's ears. Curious stares permeated the room. "Blake whispered something back to the child, then stated to her openly, "I am going to carry you because I think those little feet are hurt pretty bad if that is alright with you. It's not that I don't think you are a big girl, okay."

Amber smiled and nodded her head. Blake stood up, lifting Amber in her arms. "Which way?" She asked, and Amber pointed. "We are going to take care of a little lady business if you all don't mind." Blake offered to the room, then disappeared to the bathroom with Amber and closed the door.

Slater still stood with a smirk on his face, and moments later, two women entered the front door of the house.

"I am Ms. Butler of Children Services, and this is Myra. We are here to take temporary custody of a small child with a deceased parent." Ms. Butler announced. She was a large black woman with a booming voice not unlike one that could fill a church choir solo while shaking the house. Myra was a more petite woman of an undeterminable age. She was also black with dark skin, thick glasses, and braids. Myra seemed to exist in the considerable shadow of Ms. Butler, which spoke volumes about the relationship status between the women. Before anyone could respond, there was the sound of a toilet flushing, and without moving their faces, all the police and techs in the room's eyes rolled toward the bathroom door.

"For the love of God, please tell me there is a female officer in there with her." Ms. Butler prayed. They heard toilet flushing followed by a little voice singing a hand-washing song designed to time how long the proper time is to wash the hands. First, the song was sung in English, then in French, and then in Spanish.

The door opened, and Blake exited carrying Amber. Her feet had been cleaned and wrapped in a towel.

Myra crossed the room to meet them and stated. "Hello, sweetheart, you must be Amber. I am Myra, and I am here to book you into my little people's hotel.

Now it looks like we need to stop at the doctors. I will make it as painless as possible." Amber held onto Blake as she tried to pass the child over to Myra. "Don't be afraid your friend can come visit you."

"Bonnie, do you promise you will visit me?" Amber asked.

"Most certainly will."

Blake handed her the child and then her business card. She may witness this mess, but the sergeant on duty, that is in charge of the outside; his name is Robinson, and he is a tall, good-looking guy. Make sure he knows she needs to be assigned an officer to watch over her until such a time as Major Case says otherwise."

"Well, Spencer, does that mean you are taking this one?" Slater asked.

"Well, based on this, I see why you called. As of 6:45 pm, Major Case is now taking this Case."

"Gee, Spencer, all you see here is not why I call you old buddy." Slater reached into the large envelope he had been carrying since Spencer and Blake's arrival. He presented an evidence bag with a Badge and credentials. "This identified the deceased as Patrick Boone with the FBI."

"So why didn't you call the FBI?"

He reached back into the envelope. "Because this identifies him as Patrick Boone of Homeland. And I have one that says he is with the Department of Defense."

"Fakes?"

"I hope to God so, but if they are the best fakes I have ever seen. They also have smart chips, which were just added. We know they have them. We do not have the technology to read them."

Detective Spencer was starting to make a comment when an alarm went off. It was a loud alarm, like the blaring noise from a naval vessel. The light began to flash. Everyone stood still, waiting for the next person to explain what was happening.

Suddenly, a loud woman's voice yelled over multiple speakers in the house, producing a bone-chilling echo.

WARNING. WARNING. THERE HAS BEEN A VOIOATION OF PROTOCAL.

SYSTEMS ARE SET TO RESPOND IN ONE MINUTE.

A choir of heartbeats bounded waiting until the minute elapsed.

WARNING DETONATION SEQUENCE HAS BEEN ACTIVATED. YOU HAD 15 MINUTES TO REACH MINIMUM SAFE DISTANCE.

"What the heck is that?" Slater asked.

"Must be dessert," Spencer answered.

"Oh. Oh, someone woke up Maggie. She lives in the box in the basement, and she sounds mad." Amber whispered softly.

"If you cowboys are going to blow up the neighborhood, I think it's time we leave. I'll check the news to find out how it came out." Ms. Butter announced, grabbing Myra by the arm, and ushering her and Amber through the door.

As Myra descended the stairs leading from the house with Amber in her arms, Spencer watched from the door. He somewhat expected Morgan to follow her little sister, but she did not.

She stood staring at the house.

Something in the change on her face now told Spencer she did not care that she was losing any tactical advantage she may have gained earlier in her attempt to deceive him with suggested flirting.

There was something larger now in play. Spencer knew it was Maggie.

Chapter 2 THE CONGRESSWOMAN

"Congressman Tobin, I don't give a rat's ass about a dance this late in the evening. Quite frankly, I think it is insulting and futile to argue the point further." Congresswoman JoAnn Browser Interrupted Congressman Tobin.

"Madam, you lack compassion and empathy for those less fortunate than yourself. If you could see your way clear to study the documents before you."

The session was an evening meeting in one of the conference rooms of the Whitehouse. A group of Democratic Congressmen had been trying to agree to a proposal to put before the entire session of Congress and to formulate a plan that the President would accept. Unifying the proposal would assure greater backing, elevating the chances of approval with few proposed changes from the opposition party.

"Sir, are you daft? This horseshit you are proposing is the same lame Shit you proposed five years ago. Even the punctuation has not changed. Five years ago, we let it pass as a rider on a bill we almost lost because this sneaky crap is not fooling anyone." Brower began raising her voice to the session. "We let it pass because you cried and moaned that your constituents needed time to adjust to the change. We let that ride with your plan that in three to five years, this would have died through attrition or natural causes. Now like some messiah, you come here trying to breathe new life back into this freaking mummy."

The room was an oval table with ten officials seated and a facilitator at the head of the table. As the facilitator, it was clear that Congressman Rush wanted the bickering to end. He had his own opinions but knew injecting them might prolong the battle. Two tall men in military suits entered the room with Congresswoman Browser's aids.

There were four aids: Donna, Marla, Jackie and Sam. Each carried a cell phone and looked as if the cold shock had just rocked their world.

It took a lot of work to tell if the aid were with the officers or vice versa.

"You can't interrupt these meetings," Rush announced.

"Sir, I am Coronal Ford of with the DOD, and yes, sir, I can. "One of the officers shouted back, walking across the room and facing Bowser. "National emergency."

Congresswoman Brower stared at the officer. For a moment, it looked like all the blood had rushed out of her face.

"Damn, it's Maggie, isn't it."

"Yes."

"Which one?"

"Jennings Missouri, St. Louis County."

She swallowed hard, now more aware that others in the room were watching her reaction. "How bad."

"We need to discuss this outside."

"GET ME ON A PLANE TO St. Louis. Beg, borrow, steal. I don't care if you have to buy one; I need to be there." Browser screamed into the face of Donna, the senior most aid.

"There is an emergency call from Homeland. Some guy named Dorsey." Jackie injected, and the group hurried down the hall, almost running.

"Tell Dorsey, whoever the fuck he is, I need his boss on the phone."

"He says his boss had a stroke, and until someone tells him differently, he is the boss unless you want him to contact the President."

"Assholes. I am surrounded by Assholes."

"We got you a plane. But there is a problem." Donna announced.

The group stopped cold at the announcement. "It's not commercial, exactly. The US Marshals Service is doing a secure dispatch so that it won't be the most comfortable, but it will leave in less than an hour."

"Then I suggest we high tell the hell out of here.

Chapter 3 DESSERT

"After we found the ID, we thought we would take a look and see what else we might find to give us a fix on the deceased." Office Poole began explaining. Slater, Spencer, and Blake had gone down a flight of stairs leading to the basement, and the alarm was sounding. A couple of police Poole and Nash stood like children with their hands caught in the cooking jar or more like children with their hands stuck in the cookie jar. "We flipped open the laptop." He pointed to a laptop on a box the size of a computer desk. "We wanted to know if maybe he had kiddie porn, you know, with children in the home; we thought we should check." Spencer nodded to move them along more than agreeing. "Well, this isn't really a laptop." He raised a cabinet section that revealed wires and a lighted board. There was a palm reader and optical reader and devices that were attached to the device that took a while to understand. "It's a mini main frame and a cooler."

"What the hell is a mini mainframe?" Slater asked.

"Something with no business in this house," Spencer answered.

"You might want to see this." Officer Nash had been following the wire from the mainframe and now knew where they led.

He opened a cabinet and there was a couple of hundred pounds of plastic explosive.

"Shit," Slater stated.

"Can't we just cut the blue wire or the green wire or whatever they do in the movies," Poole asked with a note of responsibility in his voice.

"No. Son, all that is Hollywood trying to build suspense.

You start tinker with that device, it will explode just as sure as I am standing here." Spencer explained. Before he could make his next point, his cell phone rang. It was Edmund Davis, head of St. Louis Major Case. "Busy evening. Lots of bodies." He reported.

"Got a bomb or anti-personal device of some sort. Looks like two hundred pounds of C4." He paused for the response. "Yeah, the new stuff. Tell the bomb squad to take their time. The thing is going off in about fifteen minutes if you can trust the counter. It looks like someone had the good sense to pack it against the main gas line in the house, so it looks like we will probably be flying over the police station on Tucker before those guys get their truck loaded. Why don't I call you back? I got some work to do. Yeah, I know good knowing you too, Sir." Slater, Blake, and the officers stared at Spencer as if he had lost his mind.

"Will you guys excuse me for a minute? I promise I'll be right back."

"SO, HOW DID I DO?"

Spencer asked Morgan. He had gone outside and rested against the police car where she was leaning. "I mean, it was a test?"

"Please don't hate me. Sometimes, I find myself trying to explain things to people who do not know what I am talking about. They want to dismiss what I am saying and chalk it up to my age. And my age doesn't matter if I am the one who has the important information. I need to know who would figure it out."

"Well, when you did not leave with your sister, I knew there was something afoot, as they say."

"I'll shut it down, but there are conditions."

"Do I look like I am in a position to negotiate?"

"Still, in the interest of fair play, you need to know the terms of your unconditional surrender." She smiled. The sexual playfulness had reentered her eyes.

"Go. We have less than ten minutes before this county of a smoldering hole in the ground."

"First, I shut her down my way, don't ask; that's part of the condition. Second, I get to see my sister as soon as you can arrange it. On that, I will trust you. And last, when you meet my mother, and you will, you promise you won't let her corrupt you." Morgan then did what looked like baseball or football hand signals before starting for the house. Spencer had no idea who or what she had gestured to but that he knew he would be dealing with later.

"GOOD EVENING, MAGGIE."

Moran and Spencer had joined the officers in the basement.

"Good evening, Operator Morgan. How was today's run?" Maggie asked.

"I think I was a little slow and off my personal record."

"No, you are mistaken operator. You added ninety seconds, but your most recent runs for the same or similar distances have been on flat ground. You are moving faster, and your selected incline is helping you build the speed you will need for the charity run."

"This is unreal. Is she really having a conversation with the computer, and it is challenging her answer?" Bonnie asked as if everyone else in the room understood what was happening better than she.

"Status report." Morgan requested.

"Five minutes and twenty-eight seconds and it is Kaboom," Maggie answered. "Do you wish to abort the command?"

"Negative. I wish to alter to command." The group looked at Spencer, wondering if he knew something they did not.

"Your current directive is one seven four zero one. Confirm."

Maggie confirmed the code.

Maggie confirmed the current directive as instructed.

"Alter current directive to one seven five zero seven. Repeat."

"The new directive is set to be one seven five zero seven. Currently, I am challenging your decision to alter the detonation." A round of stares circulated the small basement. Did the computer challenge the command to turn itself off? There was a look of total disbelief on Poole and Nash's faces. Spencer had a confident look as if he understood what was happening.

"Challenge excepted." Morgan announced.

"Please place your right hand over the palm scanner." Maggie requested.

Morgan's hand was scanned. "Now repeat after me. Mary had a little lamb." Maggie instructed.

"Mary had a little lamb." Morgan stated.

"Again"

"Mary had a little lamb."

"I got to ask, what's that all about," Slater asked Spencer, hoping he had the answer.

"It is doing more than identifying her as the person with the permission to change the command. It's doing a comparative stress analysis using her voice. Just in Case someone has a gun to her head telling her to shut it down." He answered.

"I have heard about such software, but this is amazing. And it has no business in this house either."

The alarm stopped, and the computer started to pop and click and make disk-spinning sounds. "It's going to take her a few minutes to complete the download and wipe the drive, but after the emails are sent, she won't be a problem."

Chapter 4 ON BOARD THE PLANE

"Do you mind sitting downwind? Whatever that God awful stuff is that your generation of would-be Casanova's if using for cologne is choking me and giving me a headache." Browser complained to Dorsey. Dorsey was as muscular, good-looking man with harden chiseled features. His pearly with teeth and poster boy smile emanated and showed him to be a rising star. He had hitchhiked a ride on the plane to St. Louis. Bowser was taking every possible opportunity to harass him.

"Are you calling your hairdresser?" Brower asked Jackie. Jackie was one other young congressional aide for the Congresswoman. She was huddled in the corner using a satellite phone that had been provided by the marshals lending the travel space to the Congresswoman.

Jackie was a graduate of a military academy and the female boxing champ for her unit in the military. The assignment to the Congresswoman was a steppingstone, and they both knew it. Since Browser could only push her around with limits in her usual caustic way, from time to time, she liked to test the waters.

"That was my contact in the St. Louis Police Department. The news is not good. They have pulled at least four dead bodies from an address in Jennings. Major Case has been called in. It sounds like a shit storm where we are headed." Jackie reported.

"I got some good news. The clock on the detonation has been stopped. Maggie is in something called one seven five zero seven, whatever that is." Dorsey reported as he checked his messages. "Whatever that is."

"Young, old, male or female? Jackie, if you can find that out, it will mean a lot." Browser offered the first thing from her mouth that did not sound like a threat or insult. "And can someone find me a whiskey. And please stop referring to that damn computer as if it is a person."

"I'm an aid Congresswoman, not a cocktail waitress."

"But you would look cute in one of those outfits with that ass. So please try shaking it in front of someone that knows where they hide Shit on this death trap and see if you can't find me something for medicinal purposes."

"Mother, I don't think they serve alcohol on the US Marshals plane." Marla explained. Marla was an aide but also Browser's adopted daughter. Congresswoman had married Marla's father when Marla was very young, and the now Congresswoman was on her way up the ladder. Marla's father had been a Washington mover and shaker and wanted no place in the direct political spotlight. He was not one for having his personal life monitored. He did have the power and pushed to install his wife.

"Baby, even Captain Kirk kept a bottle of Romulan brandy around for medicinal purposes. Surely these humps can sacrifice their private stock.

It's either that or find a fly-through liquor store."

"I'll ask." She answered, scurrying off. The other aids eyed Marla, knowing she was unqualified for her position, but if your mom is the queen, that's all it takes.

Chapter 5 THE SHOOT OUT ON HIGHWAY 70

Spencer dove east on highway 70 from the scene at the house in Jennings. It was a mess when he left with barricade and yellow tape everywhere, but he knew this part of the job was being left in good hands. Detective Blake sat next to him, looking at information on the onboard computer.

Morgan sat in the back seat.

"Where is your brother?"

Spencer called back to Morgan.

"He's around. Papa's his hero." She stopped at what might have been a revealing comment.

The screen went blank on the computer in the police cruiser.

"Can you use your cell phone?" Morgan asked Blake.

She checked. "That's funny. The damn thing went dead."

"They're coming. You may want to give me a gun." Morgan yelled.

"What the?" And before Spencer could finish his statement, his cruiser was rammed from the side by a large Black Suburban. Another identical Suburban pulled up behind him and started, forcing the car into the media.

There was slammed and tires started squealing as the police cruiser struggled to maintain itself. "They use jammers to block all signals before the strike. About that gun." Morgan reiterated.

Before they could decide on the next move, the car had been flipped by the Suburban. The cruisers lie upside down. Spencer crawled from the reck and pulled his weapon. A 9mm Glock 19. Blake seemed to bound out of the car with her gun in hand. Blake had been a college track and field champ, and her being in shape was being put to the test. It was unclear at first where Morgan was. A light mist started, and visibility started getting worse quickly.

There was plenty of traffic on the Highway, and it was unclear if anyone driving could notice what was happening.

Men starting down the incline that made of the side of the Highway all checking their AK 47s.

Chapter 6 THOMAS JEROME BOONE OR JUST TJ FOR SHORT

TJ drove following the police cruiser as it left the house in Jennings. With all the emergency vehicles parked in front of his house, it would have been hard to get closer. Morgan had texted him orders. Sometimes, it's just good not to be the one in charge. He noticed the large Suburban's with the blacked-out windows and the particular interest they seem to be showing in the cruiser. He thought maybe they are surveillance, and no one will be hurt. When the SUVs started crashing into the police cruiser, he knew time was of the essence. TJ was driving the Dodge Hellcat that belonged to his father. On the first impact with the police cruiser from the SUV, TJ accelerated full out and drove past the crash and to the next ramp. He doubled back and saw the overpass above the crash site. One hundred yards piece of cake, he thought. He snatched the bag he carried from the truck. He almost lost his footing as he climbed over the guard rail to the muddy ground parallel to the crash site. He had been taught to assemble the M110A1 in the dark. He had to beat his record time to save his sister.

The snipper rifle comes with a suppressor to help keep the sound down, and it also reduces the flash. He loaded the 7.60x51mm NATO rounds and began the sight adjustment. This type of shooting is usually done by a two-man team. And usually there is time to set up a nest, but not tonight. At one hundred yards, it could be done. He was aware of the down draft being caused by the speeding cars on the Highway and knew there could be no extra shots. Each shot had to count for something. He set his sight line if they cross this point they die.

ONE OF THE MEN IN TACTICAL clothes opened fire on the car, and it caught flames. When the man went to switch magazines, Spencer rose slightly and shot him through the goggles. Another man seemed to get an exact fix on Spencer, but before he could adjust, Bonnie shot him in the thigh. He went down on his knees, and she shot him in the face. There was a scurrying in the mud alongside the disaster, and it was Morgan. She has retrieved a small piece of glass from the rear-view mirror and had a small handgun.

Morgan turned her back to the men, used the glass as a mirror, shot a small gun over her shoulder, and shot one of the men in the head. Blake and Spencer looked at each other in total amazement. The man who had just had his head blown off staggered back into the Highway, and a truck hit him. The truck laid on the brakes, but the stop time for an 18-wheeler was not a split second, so the body bounced and hit the grill of the truck a second time. The ragged corpse landed in the center lane, and cars started crashing into one another.

Trying to avoid the ragged, bloody, partial human mess that flew in all directions and now shot spray of blood and body parts everywhere.

Three of the tactical team made a rush for the three stranded between the car fire and the highway traffic, but they crossed TJ's imaginary line.

One of the men's head exploded as the snipper round hit it. The tactical team members looked startled to a point of being frozen in their tracks.

Then a second man's head exploded a plumb of pinkish spray caused by the heat from the round being cooled by the evening drizzle rose. The spray of blood, guts and brain matter flumed through the air and sprayed on Spencer, Blake, and Morgan.

"What the hell is that?" Blake screamed.

The remaining men from the tactical team seemed to get the message and ran back to the SUVs. A sniper round hit one of the SUVs and seemed to go through the vehicles and pass straight through. It shattered a window on exiting that cover with blood before shattering and crashing to the ground.

"Cover fire. A snipper, and damn is he good." Spencer answered.

The SUVs took off and drove, cashing into many of the cars that were part of the multi-car pile-up that covered the east Highway. Cars started crashing into one another in the westbound lanes as looky lous gawked and misjudged the cars around them.

Spencer, Blake, and Morgan stood watching the police cruiser burn and the attack squad survivors escaped. A police car with its lights flashing appeared on the outer road on the south rim of the Highway. The car stopped and a uniformed St. Louis City policeman got out. He climbed the small metal fence that bordered the Highway, landed in the mud, then collected himself and ran down the hill toward the small group.

"Shit. You guys must be the missing Major Case folks."

The acknowledgement came from a short, muscular policeman whose man tag read Casper. "You guys sure know how to throw a party." He added, looking at the multi-car pile that had now overtaken both sides of the Highway. "How do I join up?"

"May I?" Spencer requested, holding out his hand and looking at the radio the policeman carried. "What cop is on the Shreve Street over pass." Spencer called into the radio. There was no response. Morgan smiled slightly, and she heard the roar of the Hellcat roared in the distance.

Mission accomplished, little brother, she thought.

"Where did you get the gun?" Blake asked, snatching the gun from her.

"My grandmother gave to me."

"Smart ass."

Chapter 7 GET READY FOR THE MEETING

"I got us checked into the Airport Marriott. It's right across from the airport where we are landing. I am planning for vehicles and setting a meeting with Deputy Chief Edmund Davis, who runs major Case." Jackie announced, happily that someone had found a dusty old bottle of some no-name whiskey during the flight to quiet the Congresswoman, so some work could be done. Marla had sat across from her adopted mother, removed her shoes, and massaged the Congresswoman's feet, which caused the Congresswoman to drift off into sleep. Donna, Marla, Jackie, and Sam the aids all seem to notice that the Congresswoman wept silently in her sleep. The looked amongst themselves only secure in the knowledge that they did not wish to discuss it and that wherever the personal hardship or loss imbedded in her soul it had made her what she now was.

Chapter 8 ASSEMBLE THE TEAM

"Alright, guys, here's the way it works. Blake and I have the hot hand. That means we are the primary of the hottest thing going on. So, keep in mind that even though Blake has fewer years of service than most of any of you, if you disrespect her, it's the same as disrespecting me. Are we clear on that?" Spencer was using his leadership voice. This commanding tone inspired many of his fellow Detective because they knew he had experience.

"She has less time on the planet than any of us, but we are with you." Detective Yolanda Red Smith confirmed as she stood behind her partner, Lamont Franklin. Yolanda went by the name Red because she was a black woman with a light complexion.

Yolanda was known for getting her work done but also for having a jovial nature that had a way of coming in hand with complex cases. Her partner Lamont Franklin was an enormous dark-skinned black man who, when you looked at him, you wondered why he wasn't playing nose guard on a pro football team; he had shiny black skin like the paint job on an overpriced sports car. He had a shiny bald head, and Yolanda stood behind him pretending to fix her hair using the reflection from his head.

"Don't take this the wrong way, but why are you, too, still alive? The report for the traffic helicopter says a death squad pinned you down with AK-47s and on the way out?" Detective Walter Graves asked, trying to thumb through a copy of the report that Blake had prepared.

Graves's Partner was Kate Smith. Smith and Graves had always made great partners. They were family-orientated and did not believe in social flirting or any form of distraction that might cause an emotional misunderstanding. On numerous occasions, Graves had made it clear to members of the opposite sex that an unwelcome comment to or about his partner was an insult to him, and she and had occasion the do the same for him.

"There was a sniper out there that backed us," Blake noted, pointing to the section in the report.

"Bullshit." Yolanda started, then thought about how it sounded. "Sorry. I mean rain and with bad to no visibility, flashing lights from the highway, not to mention the downdraft from the cars traveling 65 miles an hour."

"That's not the spooky part. There were three shots. I do long-distance shooting. Three shots are bad from a single point because an expert, such as Spencer, can make your location." Graves added.

Everyone but Blake seemed to get his point, so Spencer cleared it up.

"Military-grade suppressor, expensive scope and reduction of flash and some system to compensate for drop per distance as adjustment for altitude as well as to adjust for humidity." The gun didn't come from a hobby shop. "We are talking about a 10,000-dollar shooting system."

"Say if we find this guy, can we at least see if he needs a job? Of course, he will probably have to wear a kilt because his balls are too big for pants." Yolanda added. "And he better be good to my big monkey." She stated, hugging Detective Franklin from behind. They all sat in the corner of the office. The section the detectives had chosen was a few desks away from distraction from the other offices and the people they were being processed. Yolanda picking on Franklin caught everyone's attention.

"Is that necessary?" Spencer asked.

"Yes, Sir, we had a bet, and he lost. I get to refer to him as my big monkey for two weeks since he lost."

"What would he have gotten if he won?" Blake asked.

"An executive lap dance." She stopped rubbing Franklin's head and spoke. "That's right, you come from Alabama, so you probably haven't heard of that. It's a lap dance where I wear nothing but a wet undershirt. No panties. And he is handcuffed to the chair." She started gyrating to demonstrate the activity in question.

"Oh my." A grin overtook Blake's face.

"Man, I would have shot the Pope for that dance," Franklin confessed. The room took on a round of laughter. When Franklin raised his head, he saw Deputy Chief Edmund Davis staring at him.

"I realize it's only ten o'clock in the morning, folks, but I am glad we are only planning to kill people this morning after the events of yesterday. And it is good to see you putting together a team. Spencer and Blake, if you can join me in thirty minutes in the main conference room, we will be joined by guests who would like a recap of the Wild West show we are now running."

Blake went back to passing out an assignment to the offices to be sure they were covering the correct areas. Checking ballistics and ME reports. He was studying for the license for the vehicle's registration. Checking the authenticity of the credentials for the various government agencies found at the scene and ensuring all involved would be kept in the loop. It was the way Spencer had taught her. And she was proud to be his student even if she was unclear why it made people uncomfortable that he had taken on another female partner. She also noticed two men in suits she did not recognize watching her.

At first, she thought it was just men watching women, but they were carrying large folders and seemed to be looking through her. They started walking toward her. "Blake?" one of the men, an older balding man in a suit that looked like he slept in, asked. Yolanda noticed the men and rushed to stand beside Blake.

"Michael's Internal Affairs Shooting Review." He announced.

Yolanda eyed the men, knowing who they were. "She's clean as a preacher's sheets."

"Your Deputy chief wants us to bypass the formalities and keep you on the case you are working. He feels we are under a time crunch to get ahead of some bad press. The mayor and the Governor would like to have a favorable resolution, as soon as possible."

"I say fuck politics." The other man, a tall officer with no facial expression, interjected.

"Sir, we were on the highway at night being attacked by a bunch of guys with machine guns. Frankly, I didn't even know machine guns were common in St. Louis. I had to defend myself. My partner and the civilian were transporting to see her minor-aged sister who was being seen by a doctor for broken glass cuts to her feet."

Both internal affairs detectives looked at each other with the look of ultimate boredom. They had her sign a form and were off to find better prey.

Chapter 8 THE MEETING IN THE CONFERENCE ROOM

Spencer and Blake knew being called somewhere other than the Deputy Chief's office for a meeting meant there was something important about the meeting. The hint that there would be guests was quite the tip them off, but it did not brace them for the group they saw headed for the conference room. Morgan had been offered a room at a local chain hotel by victim assistance. At the same time, her primary place of residence was being processed as a crime scene. Spencer had her brought to the police station for a question-and-answer session with the hopes of getting a better handle on the events unfolding. Morgan sat on a small bench with a young man who looked just a little younger than she. The young man had a buzz cut that would make the Marines proud. No piercing or visible tattoos and a clean, fresh, scrubbed look the mothers hoped their daughters would someday bring home. He was also a younger version of the homeowner they had seen lying dead on the floor of the house in Jennings. This had to be TJ. Morgan held her arm through his in a fashion that made it difficult to tell who was supporting whom. If there was sibling rivalry or petty disputes between these two, it was not on hold or permanently called on account of grief.

"I am going into a meeting. I don't want to be disturbed unless it's the White House." Davis said sarcastically to Joy Alexander, the civilian receptionist who doubled as his secretary during busy periods.

"Sure."

In his mind, Spencer debated bringing TJ and Morgan into the meeting with him, then thought it might be a good idea. Then, if there were matters that did not involve them, they could be sent out. If they knew about what had transpired, it would be of greater value than jurisdictional squabbling.

"Congresswoman Browser and her aids, Department of Defense Major Bradley, Mr. Dorsey Homeland, Mr. Sanford Lowell, an attorney for the Congresswoman, Randy Gibbs, you may know he is with the Marshals office and is handling the security for the congresswoman." Edmund Davis began introducing people as Spencer entered the room with Blake, Morgan, and TJ. "FBI Shannon Reed, Missouri District Attorney's office Newton and Fed District Attorney's office. Have I missed anyone?"

"First, let me say I feel that it is insulting that the FBI must crash a meeting that, by all practical purposes, is most likely our case. I don't know that you have the time, the manpower, or, quite frankly, the brain power to handle something of this scope." Reed announced as all found seats.

Major Bradley, a tall man in a crisp uniform, reached over the table to shake Morgan and TJ's hands. "Let me say first." He stopped and took a long stare at Reed. "I am sorry for your loss. I hope you are being treated well under the circumstances. I am a family man, and my concern is with you." A moment of quiet reflection swept the room. "Miss Boone, I would like to personally thank you for your reports and for securing sensitive information." A slight shock wave seemed to ripple through the room, but not everyone was caught in it; some knew what he was praising. "Thomas J Boone, I have gotten nothing but good reports from your Uncle Buddy."

"God, how could the bastard still be alive?" The congresswoman asked.

"Does this old drunk have to be here?" Morgan asked, staring at the Congresswoman.

Before the shock of Morgan's comment could fully register, TJ made a comment that caused many in the room total confusion. "Please, Morgan, she is still our mother."

"What?" Was the only word Marla could utter.

"As interesting as this is, we are taking the computer and the explosives from your custody," Reed announced, attempting to capitalize on the confusion in the room or perhaps thinking she was the only one who did not know the relationship of Morgan and TJ to the Congresswoman.

"Sorry, counselor, it belongs to the DOD, and we have a court order."

"How could anyone have a court order that fast?" Davis asked. "And does that order say how the shit showed up in someone's private home?"

"Part of Morgan Boones shut down macro on the computer was a request to the agency owning the device and ordinance to come and reclaim their property," Spencer explained while Blake looked at him in wonder. Blake thought to herself, that's why he did not care where the bomb or computer was; he knew it was being reclaimed. Maggie was automatically sending different departments emergency emails.

"You can't put anything past this devious bitch." The Congresswoman mumbled.

"Since we have the hall and all of you good people in the same place, just a couple of fill-in-the-blank questions. Mr. Boone has several IDs for different government agencies. We can't prove any of them are fake. First question: are they fake?" Spencer looked around the room. "Jump ball people." Major Bradly nodded to Morgan. It was confirmation, and it was almost indistinguishable, but it was there.

"They are real. He was contracted, you might say, to do work for various government agencies." Morgan answered.

There was a milling around outside the meeting room, and the door was open. Joy Alexander stood in the doorway. She had wide eyes and a naturally frazzled look, but now she looked like she had seen a ghost.

"Joy, I thought I asked you not to disturb us." Edmund Davis snapped.

"No sir, you told me not to disturb you unless the White House calls. You have a call from the White House on the line and one from the Governor on a separate line."

"What have you people gotten me into." Edmund Davis looked around the room, not even expecting an answer.

Chapter 9 THINGS INSIDE THE MARRIOTT

The remainder of the meeting after Edmund Davis's return had proven less than productive. Most people wanted to defend their represented group. The FBI wanted to blame Homeland and vice versa, but neither wanted to go on record as to what exactly they were blaming the other for.

Sandford Lowell, counsel for the Congresswoman, felt that the presence of Federal and State District attorneys was somewhat out of line in a fact-finding inquiry. Deputy Chief Edmund did not go over his phone conversations verbatim upon his return to the meeting but told them that the White House Chief of Staff instructed him to continue his investigation until such time as he saw fit. Then and only then would he be assured he was putting the inquiry in the correct hands, should he feel the need to pass the examination to a federal level. The Governor, who frequently agreed with little coming out of the White House, agreed that any efforts by any group, including but not limited to the FBI, DOD, or Homeland, that tries to manipulate or bully the collection of information being collected by the investigating officers of Major Case would have to answer to the department of justice. The White House Chief of staff and the Governor's office wanted a daily report before any releases to the press. This revelation seemed to throw a damper on the strategies of most of the members of the meeting. Morgan grew hostile toward Marla anytime she was referred to as the Congresswoman's daughter.

"SO, YOU DO KEEP YOUR word." Morgan proclaimed as she stepped back to allow Myra to wheel a wheelchair containing Amber into the room at the Marriott that Morgan and TJ had been sharing.

Spencer and Blake accompanied Myra and Amber. TJ sat with his legs crossed, playing a game on a tablet. He stopped and smiled at his little sister as she was wheeled into the room. "Love you, TJ." Amber proclaimed, and a mist was caught in TJ's eyes. "Love you too, operator."

"I looked up your record for track and field online for the University of Alabama. Pretty impressive. You think you are still that fast?" Morgan asked, standing toe to toe with Blake as she entered the room. Both women had a similar body type, but Blake, at five foot seven, was a little taller and had broader shoulders, which were a sign of police academy training. Spencer walked into the room, sat in a chair, and watched two women sizing each other up like competitive athletes. "Bonnie's been good to me, Morgan. She comes to see me and brings me things." Amber announced. Morgan broke off the stare-down and began stroking Amber's hair. "Look, I am sorry. I guess I was a little keyed in the meeting. How can this bitch call someone else daughter when she abandoned us? My papa loved her to the day he died. She would make midnight booty calls. Amber used to call her the Angel that appears at night but must be gone by first light. Did that look like an angel to you?" Her comment was mostly directed toward Spencer. "I am sorry. Without anyone telling me anything, we are bound to make some missteps. I never would have guessed. But it does tell me where we need to start."

"Do tell." TJ looked up, smiling at Morgan's skepticism.

"Sure, let's start with the obvious. What did your father do, and let's skip the private contractor various agency nonsense? I don't think they send death squads after secretaries or janitors." Spencer asked.

"Can she step out into the hall?" Morgan asked, looking at Myra but not addressing her directly.

"Amber has not yet been released. I have to stay with her."

"Please, Myra, we will take total responsibility." Blake offered to escort the young woman to the door. Myra left with a look of defeat on her face.

"He was a mole hunter." Morgan began. "After 9/11, it was clear that there were people doing things that compromised national security. Not just the Middle East but also here at home, the fragmented state of US intelligence created a significant void, and we were leaking valuable info like a sieve." Morgan looked up to be sure they were following before proceeding. "People could steal small bits of info that seemed not to be harmful, but if other pieces were being stolen by someone else, then put together, the trouble was massive." Spencer and Blake looked at each other, noticing how the transformation in Morgan was clearly apparent. Morgan now looked and sounded more like the operator the Major from the DOD had been showing total respect for in the meeting.

"How deep are you guys in this?" Blake asked.

"Usually, I write reports and manage updates," Morgan answered. "Dull, boring stuff."

"There, and we were being so honest." Spencer mocked. "I saw the Annie Oakley shooting, and it would be my guess that was TJ with the snipper riffle, and even Amber knows which end of the knife is the business end. You texted TJ before we took off and told him to ensure we got to the police station."

"I did puzzles with little Amber on my visits. She likes them. The thing is a group of leading psychologists developed the puzzles I was giving here to measure IQ. They are most effective with children because the child is being tested without knowledge, so the reading is more accurate. Amber completes puzzles on an intelligence level twice her age. I got the idea when we were washing our hands together, and she sang in different languages." Blake announced.

"Busted." TJ laughed without looking up from his game.

"Well, I guess it's time you guys left to get some rest. You have a big day tomorrow. You will meet our Uncle Buddy, and it's a long drive. See you guys at Eight AM sharp." Morgan explained.

Myra wheeled Amber into the elevator, followed by Spencer and Blake, as they left the third-floor hotel room occupied by Morgan and TJ.

Myra went to press the first-floor button, and Spencer caught her arm. "We're going up." He pushed the six-floor button. As the door opened, Jackie, one of the Congresswoman's aids, and Major Bradley stood ready to enter the elevator. They both smiled and pushed past those exiting the elevator.

"Well. Well." Blake commented. "Let's not jump to conclusions, Detective," Spencer suggested, checking the directory showing the directions of the room numbers. Myra smiled, not saying anything. Marla answered the door with a look of amazement on her face. The Congresswoman stood behind her in a bathrobe. "I am not used to meeting folks in a bathrobe, but I did not plan this trip, and my kids are out scouring the world for appropriate attire. Hopefully, the Salvation Army is open." Commented, holding a drink in one hand. The Congresswoman reached for Amber, but Blake blocked her with her body. "I am sorry, but Myra and Amber will remain in the hallway as some of the topics and the flow of adult beverages are not a suitable environment for a child her age.

I am sure you will agree."

"Where did you pick up that horrible fucking accent?" The Congresswoman baited Blake in retaliation.

"Marla, will you please join Amber and Myra in the hall? We only had a few questions."

"Mother, would you like for me to contact a lawyer?"

"No one is arresting anyone. They are just having trouble finding their way in the dark. Isn't the right Mr. Spencer?"

"Detective Spencer." Blake corrected.

"Can I offer either of you a drink? Surely, if anyone looked like they needed to lighten up, it is you two."

"People's heads exploding does that to some folks, I reckon." Blake responded.

"Look here, country girl, I loved that man with all my heart. I did not shed a single tear when my second husband died, and you know why?

Because I never loved him. He loved me, and that was the basis of our relationship. Patrick was different. He was the best part of me. My second husband had a vasectomy long before we met. All three of those children from that home you went to are mine." Her eyes filled with tears, but her face still mainly showed anger. "Now they hate me, and this is my legacy."

"Did you have control of his projects?" Spencer sought to take advantage of her need to talk.

"At one point, I ran the missions. I'll give you a little example of what you are asking about, my dear Detective." She paused and poured herself another drink and almost fell into the chair seating herself. "Some time ago in Bosnia or some other ethnic cleansing cesspool, some shithead got the idea to extract a bunch of young women and train them to look and act like ladies.

They released the women in DC and other places where these women attached themselves to politicians and businesspeople. Hell, the project worked so well that many of the men knew they were being used and were in too deep. They had families with these women."

"My dear departed ex-husband went to work and rooted these people out." She took a stiff drink. "Another time, a government agency took out a nest of drug smugglers in the California hills. The only problem was that they weren't really drug smugglers; they were DEA undercover.

And the whole lot of them were exterminated when the smoke cleared. So, I strongly suggest that the two of you get a room in this fine hotel and hump each other's brains out and pretend you are saving the world because the enemy you are looking for most likely salutes the same fucking flag you do."

"What is Uncle Buddy's function?"

"Training. Have you noticed how well-trained those kids are? Programed is a better word."

"They weren't just after Patrick Boone. They were there to wipe out the family." Blake realized.

"That damn Buddy creates soldiers that don't look like soldiers. That is what he does best. I have been hoping for years he died of some God-awful and painful malady. Maybe something with burning pustules or is skin completely flaking off, but apparently God had been busy elsewhere." She revealed, pouring herself another drink.

"I think that is about all we will cover today. We appreciate your time." Spencer announced, not sure she understood him as the drink overtook her.

"Anything she said in there, you can't hold it against her, and you can't talk to the press about it. She is on several vital committees." Marla pounced on them as they were leaving the room and entered to assess her adopted mother.

"WELL, THE COPS." SAM, the other aide to the Congresswoman, came toward Spencer, Blake, Myra, and Amber as they headed down the hall. He was carrying a large bag. Sam was gay and proud of it. He was attractive and well-kempt. He also made it a point to say little lest he draw unwelcome assessments from people; he did care what they thought. "I hear this place has a great nightlife for the single gay crowd." He spouted to Spencer and Blake. "They had me out shopping. I guess they figured out you can't just jump up and go hundreds of miles for an unspecified time with just the clothes on your back. I'm an aid, not a pioneer." He continued past them hurriedly to complete his tasks to free up some of his time.

"Detective Spencer, could I talk to you privately for a second?" Blake asked, motioning Spencer out of the hearing range of Myra and Amber.

"Is there a problem?" He asked.

"Well, you know how I like to keep reports accurate and put everything I can remember in them?"

"Yes. I always appreciate that."

She whispered. "Do you think I can leave out the part about her suggesting we get a room and do the whatever's to each other?"

He looked at her, trying to keep straight, but slowly failed.

"I think the report will be just as accurate if we leave that out."

She started to walk and then stopped. "It's not that if you were to ask me, I wouldn't be proud to consider something like that, but that is not something that should be showing up in an official police report. And the way Red is riding poor Lamont Franklin, I don't know I could survive an assessment that personal."

"I see your point." He whispered back.

"Just out of curiosity, would you ever try to make that type of bet with me?"

"No. If you were inclined to do a lap dance, I would want to know it has nothing to do with a bet or dare. For my own personal comfort."

"Glad we had this chat." She took a deep breath.

IN A ROOM ON THE FIFTH floor of the same hotel, Donna shoved Dorsey against the room door as he entered. The room was dim, and it was clear the atmosphere was set for their assignation.

She began kissing his neck as she struggled to remove his suit coat. "Fuck that old bitch, I love this cologne." She lied, sniffing him. She knew she chose the overbearing cologne because it would be easy to detect when he strayed. Donna began unbuttoning his shirt. "You know, if you have chosen a better assault team, this shit wouldn't be happening."

"Any better team would have had questions and sent up a red flag. Those low-budget mercenaries only blew the time by less than ten minutes.

It they had waited ten minutes later they would have got the whole family. They should have showed up after Morgan had completed her run. They should have got the whole family." Dorsey confessed.

Donna slid her hand along his bare chest and unfastened his belt.

She slipped her hand into his pants and began rubbing, and she pressed her body against his. "This is mine. All mine. Not to say I am not willing to share it. But when you do, I want to be there." She dropped to her knees and began her technique. Dorsey tried to answer, but the only sound he could utter was a throaty, primitive moan. "So, you agree." She confirmed.

MARLA ENTERED THE ROOM she and her stepmother were sharing, still upset about having been dismissed. She retrieved a sleeping pill and gave it to the Congresswoman, who still sat in the chair. Marla handed the Congresswoman a glass of water to take the mild sleeping pill. Marla then sat on the floor, took the Congresswoman's hand, and held it. She placed her head in the Congresswoman's lap like a small child. "Please tell me the truth. No lies or half-truths. I have been there for you even when my father didn't treat you well." Marla held her head up, and it was clear she was crying uncontrollably.

"The truth started a long time ago when I was about your age. I was in the army, and no matter what I did right, I could not get the promotion. So, I compromised by principles. And I gave an officer a blow job." Marla wiped her eyes and stared transfixed at the Congresswoman. "After that, it became easier and easier to compromise myself in the name of upward mobility." The Congresswoman's recitation seemed like a haunting recreation she was reliving and had relived over and over. "Then, one day, I met Patrick Boone. The kindest man I ever knew."

"Did he make you compromise further?" Marla asked.

"No, just the opposite. He taught me to respect myself and to hold my head up." She took a deep breath. "But old habits die hard if, in fact, they ever die." She paused as if to place the following words. "That's when I met Ronald, your father. He offered me a kingdom of gold, and I took it. The only price was my soul. My children and the man that saved me."

"Mother, that youngest child would have been born when you married Daddy."

The Congresswoman began stroking Marla's hair. "Your father was aware of my sexual relationship with Patrick after he became my ex-husband. You see, your father had a vasectomy after you were born."

"How could he stand to share you with another man?"

"Sometimes the strongest marriages are held together by offsetting indiscretions."

"It seems your father preferred young boys but needed a wife on his arm. I was free to go and spend a weekend occasionally as long as I looked the other way." Marla looked shocked.

"You see, the only good thing that came out of that marriage was me embracing you as my daughter. Your eyes were so innocent that I thought maybe when I stared into your eyes, I could find forgiveness for the children I had abandoned."

"Was it you that tried to kill them?"

"No. They were fine in their father's world."

Both women sat together for a time, unsure what other words could soften the harshness of the truths that had flowed through the room. There was no pretense of strength from either, only an unspoken compromise. A truce of sorts to breathe and digest the bitterness.

Chapter 10 UNCLE BUDDY'S HOUSE

"Stand still and hold your badges out in your right hands." Morgan instructed Spencer and Blake. Spencer, Blake, TJ and Morgan stood on the side of an unmarked road where Morgan had led them. The road was just outside Winona, Mississippi, a town of about 34 square miles comprised of 4500 people. The town is at the intersection of I-55 and Highway 82. When Morgan had suggested that the best way to find out what was happening was to visit Uncle Buddy, frankly, since the area is 404 miles outside of his department's jurisdiction, he figured Edmund would never agree to the trip. And even if he did, since Uncle Buddy was not a favorite of the current governmental system, he would not accept the request for the interview. He was wrong on both counts. The drive had taken close to 6 hours with two rest stops. Spencer had driven most of the way, then Blake insisted that she be allowed some time behind the wheel. This was partially her attempt to put in the second bathroom break since it was clear that men did not require the same number of rest stops as women. By the time she made up her mind to insist on a turn at the wheel, the rest stop was non-negotiable.

A large drone showed up and hovered above them. The drone had obvious camera capabilities and hovered briefly, then flew off.

"Pretty neat security," Morgan commented. A jeep drove up with a teenage girl at the wheel and a young man slightly older.

The young man was carrying a shotgun.

"Good to see you two clowns, follow us.?" The young man commented, looking at Morgan and TJ."

Spencer, Blake, Morgan, and TJ returned to the cruiser and followed the Jeep. It was clear that the police cruiser was not designed for the terrain and was taking beating as it bounced and sprang through dents, ruts, and ground that was just not made for comfort.

They were led to a small cluster of houses, with one house larger than the rest positioned in the center. A large black man stood on the front porch beside a heavy-set middle-aged woman who wore spectacles that hung on her nose. Spencer's height is about 6'2, and the man on the porch stood at least four inches taller. He had a balding head and grey facial stubble. The man on the porch was holding a small child, about 3 or 4 years old, who appeared much smaller, being helped by the giant. Buddy had a scar that had healed poorly on his neck where his throat had been cut, and the medical resources were apparently not readily available. He had a spent mark on his right cheek. The pattern a bullet makes when passing through someone's cheek.

"Nice to meet you two. I am Buddy, and this is Violet."

Buddy announced, holding out his large hand. They took turns shaking his hand.

"We will be serving a meal shortly. Violet will show you to your rooms."

"We did not come here to put you out. We just had a few questions."

Spencer announced.

"I see. You traveled over Four Hundred miles, and my wife would like you to join us in a civil meal. Surely, Sir, you did not travel Four Hundred miles to insult my wife."

"I'd take him up on the meal. Otherwise, it might mean a duel." Morgan joked, and TJ laughed.

"We would be happy to join you and your wife, Sir, frankly, I am hungry enough to eat my own arm," Blake stated.

"Whereabouts in Alabama are you from, little lady?" Buddy asked.

"Oak Hill."

"I spent time assigned to Alabama years ago. Some pretty country. So unspoiled. Isn't the town less than one hundred people?"

"Population 28."

"Oh my God," Violet exclaimed.

"I guess your wife must be from a big city." Blake offered.

Buddy reared back and laughed. "Violet's not my wife. You could say she runs the place."

Buddy turned and walked into the house with an unstated the conversation if over now; follow me that so many large people seem to have a natural commanding way. The inside of the house had a huge sunken living room with a large brown piano at one end. A small girl of five or so sat at a piano, looking at them as they entered. She was seated beside an older woman who was obviously the teacher and did not appreciate the distraction. There were four sofas facing each other, and there seemed to be children of various ages playing games and taunting each other. Interaction alone did not call out wife to husband or children to a specific parent. They all seemed to be a circle of kin. Pictures were covering all the walls. It was easy to tell that many people in the photographs were the same person at various ages. In some, you could see them as children and follow the picture through where that same person had married and or joined the armed services.

"I hate to be rude, but if you two do not mind a little business, that must be cleared up." Buddy announced to Spencer and Blake before walking over and facing Morgan. "Permission to hug you, Sir."

"Permission granted." A woman's voice announced as a pregnant woman in her early twenties appeared. The woman had a child on her hip and another toddler being led by the other hand. She was beautiful with the natural glow of a woman who was in love with being pregnant.

"This, my dear Detectives, is my wife, Tara Lynn," Buddy announced seconds before Morgan threw herself on him in a hug.

"Now, Operator Morgan, that damn Maggie is in the research room, and your attention is required."

"She didn't destroy it. She moved it." Blake said to Spencer, who clearly knew the computer's memory had been moved.

Morgan fled the room, making sure not to step on any of the children and stopping to hug a few that held up their hands in request. Buddy walked close to TJ. "Operator Thomas Jerome Boone."

TJ snapped to attention.

There was a slight tapping by the piano teacher, and the little girl started playing the piano. The little girl played Music Box Dancer. "Pick of the temp." The teacher instructed. "No faster." The girls had started moving at an incredible speed and repeated the tune. "You are almost there, my love." With this last command, the little girl ran the notes perfectly at an incredible speed. She closed her eyes and swayed.

If it is possible, she seemed to become part of the music. The little girl swayed, and the music seemed to flow through her and permeate the room, capturing any that was within range. Engulfed by the music, many of the children and adults seemed to will the young girl to more tremendous success, and it was accomplished. Every note vibrated in the hearts of the listeners. To each person, the notes were just for them and them alone.

"What is the procedure for reporting emergency field testing of a new snipper system?" Buddy asked.

"Sir."

"Don't, Sir, me answer the question."

"The Operator has 48 hours to report on the efficiency and effectiveness of the system, or he is in violation." TJ resisted.

"That being the case, it would appear that the clock is ticking, young man." Buddy scolded. Many of the children looked at the confrontation with great interest.

TJ started to walk in the direction that Morgan had disappeared.

"Are you forgetting something, young man?" Buddy asked in a booming voice.

TJ took on a tremendous grim. "Permission, Sir."

"By all means granted."

As TJ threw himself at Buddy in a hug that lifted him off his feet.

Chapter 11 THE MEAL AT UNCLE BUDDY'S FARM

"I hope it does not create too much inconvenience, but I have arranged a tour of the place. Since you two are police, I think it best to have someone show you around. This will eliminate any need for subterfuge on your part." Buddy smiled a wide grin.

A young woman named Gloria had been assigned the job as a tour guide.

She spoke fast and tried to check eye contact to verify that Spencer and Blake knew what she was presenting and to check for questions. The first stop was a large barn. The barn housed a Gym and Dojo. A short Asian man in a Karate Gi with an Olympic patch on the shoulder taught a small group of students martial arts. One end of the barn housed a boxing ring and an area with a full set of weights. There were three young girls doing yoga on mats in a corner of the building. Spencer walked without questions, but interest and amazement filled their faces.

The group walked to a small lake or pond. In the pond's center was a small boy in a fishing boat with his pole in the water. The boy looked relaxed. As the group walked around the pond, they encountered a small group of youngsters. The youngsters had easels, and it was clear that the boy in the boat was the subject of their art lesson.

"Many people think the art is about what others think of your work. Nothing could be further from the truth. True art is the evoking of a mood or feeling. It is the sharing of the mood the art passes to the viewer. Your feelings are transmitted whether you are using literature, song, or paints."

They could hear the teacher, a small blonde woman in jeans and a tee shirt, say. The woman walked over to one of the younger students and asked. "Jean, what does your representation speak?"

The young girl looked at her and, without hesitation, stated. "The boy is happy to be fishing. He does not care if he catches a fish. This is where he can think without interruption."

"I love your interpretation." The teacher commented and kissed the student on the forehead. "How about some others." She could be heard to request as Spencer, Blake, and Gloria waked out of hearing range. There was plenty to see, and Gloria moved quickly. It became clear to Spencer and Blake that it was not that she was trying to rush the tour but that she was hungry and could smell the food coming from the main house. As the small group walked, two young girls passed them. It was clear that both girls were with child. "How many wives does Uncle Buddy have?" Spencer asked. Gloria had been walking slightly in front of them, and she seemed to freeze in her tracks. She stopped and turned to Spencer. Gloria was a small girl with reddish hair. When she turned the Red in her face was twice that of her hair. "One. How many do they allow in St. Louis?"

Spencer held up his hand to make a point, but she continued. "We're not the Mormons, and we are not the Manson family. No one here is raping small children. No brothers and sisters are sleeping together.

Oh my God, did you really come hundreds of miles to insult us?" Gloria's eyes stated to form tears in the corners, and Spencer walked to her and took her arm. She was not only innocent of the things implied but had no clear emotional understanding of how such acts took place in a world beyond the one she lived in.

"Look, I am sorry. But when everything you see is so different from what you usually expect, you must ask questions. Sometimes, the general place you start is way off base. We have no desire to hurt or offend you."

She began wiping her tears. "I was assigned this duty because I knew Patrick Boone and Tera Lynn thought it might help me with some closure."

"Were you romantically involved?" Blake asked in a low voice, trying not to rattle the girl further.

"No. He did not feel it would be fair. Romantic involvements were hard for him since his marriage." She left it at that as if they understood the implication.

The remainder of the tour took a quiet tone. Blake now knew Gloria was hurting at the loss of what might have someday been.

THE SITE AT THE DINNER table was nothing short of amazing. There were too many children to count. The children were from all races and varied in age.

Blake could count at least four young girls who were pregnant. There was no squabbling, and everyone wanted to help prepare the table. There was fried chicken, mashed potatoes, and corn.

Before the meal was started, Buddy said a non-denominational blessing. "No one has to buy into a particular religion to put their feet under this table; we are as one." He commanded after the prayer, and they all feasted. At dessert, three little girls who looked like triples thought it was an excellent time to have a pie-eating contest and started stuffing their faces with blueberry pie. Tara Lynn smacked Buddy's hand playfully for watching the competition with a smirk on his face. "You don't have to encourage that type of foolishness, dear husband." She stated then noticed that Spencer also seemed to be enjoying the event.

After the meal, Spencer and Blake sat facing Buddy and Tara Lynn.

Tara Lynn was breastfeeding an infant and rubbing the back of another nestled close to her for attention.

A toddler with a weighted dipper crawled to Blake and pulled himself up.

"Honey, if you pass me that diaper bag, I can get this for you." Blake offered to Tara Lynn. It was clear Tara Lynn appreciated the gesture. Blake began changing the dipper with the most natural of motions as if she did this all the time. The toddle seemed to enjoy it as he played with his feet."

"I am sorry for your loss." Spencer began. There was the sound of a riffle being fired in the distance.

"That's Henry and TJ. Henry is testing the new HK417.

Henry is a little older than TJ, but the boys are close. It saddens me that we won't have Henry much longer. He is enlisting in the Marine Corps, and he is marrying one of our girls, Jennifer."

Buddy noted the distraction that seemed to catch Spencer's attention.

"What is this place, if I might ask?" Blake asked.

"I believe it is an experiment that people abandoned—or lost sight of. Then, later, they found a use for some of it and tried to find ways to salvage it. How do you salvage children that you dispose of?" Tara Lynn answered. "How is Amber?"

"Amber is amazing. She was in the house at the time of the attack, and she is being evaluated. It is best to know as soon as possible if she is going to need some special help." Spencer answered.

"Do you know what caused the attack?"

"Sure, don't you. I wrote reports on this ten years ago. Government sibling rivalry is the best way to describe it. Branches competing at such a clip that the only way that could be funding was to make other agencies look bad. And it is not systemic of all government. But the government is made up of people. And people hate to fail. And when one group cheats and makes the other look bad, it's only a matter of time until this type of thing happens."

"The Congresswoman thinks you are building super soldiers."

Buddy laughed, and Tara Lynn joined him. "That's old news. The first generation was that and more, but it was defunded and fell apart. The children brought their children home to this ranch, and those children became the new teachers. What you see now are children who grew and had families and were afraid that someone might come and destroy their family because of what it knew or had learned to do; you think of us as a forgotten tribe? No missions, no war to fight, only the laughter of a very big family. They harbor only goodness and kindness and a shared love for one another." Buddy explained.

"You are saying another government agency sponsored the home attack." Blake attempted to clarify.

"Look at how governments fight. They send out troops and eliminate their enemy." Tara Lynn added.

"Forgive me for saying, but this sounds like conspiracy thinking," Spencer added. "Do you train the children to kill?"

The harshness of the questions hung in the air. Like all harsh questions, not only the answer but also the ease and time it takes to answer were factored in.

"Some are taught to protect and defend. Many of the children are musicians, mathematicians, and artists. They are easy pray for people like that mercenary death squad. They must be protected. And I am sorry if the thought of a brother defending his sister is out of line with your values."

Buddy reached into his pocket and handed two pieces of paper to Spencer. "Check out these two things, and you will have your answers. It's information Patrick was working on when he was murdered. It was retrieved from Maggie. Be careful who you show that to."

Tara Lynn looked over at Blake and noticed that the toddler she was holding had attached itself to Blake's breast, attempting to extract milk through her shirt, and had made a slobbering mess of Blake's blouse. Blake was rocking the baby and did not seem to notice until the other three stared, staring at her breast.

"Little buddy, I think you are trying to pump a dry well." Tara Lynn joked as she took the toddler while carefully handing the infant she had been holding to Spencer. Buddy sat back and smiled.

Chapter 11 ANSWERS TO QUESTIONS NOT ASKED

"I owe you an apology."

Tara Lynn stated. She was showing Blake to her room for the night and getting her something to sleep in so she could clean Blake's shirt.

"No apology necessary. The little guy wasn't trying to molest me. His tiny little baby instincts kicked in, and the next thing he was doing what babies do."

"I don't mean that."

Tara Lynn looked at Blake with a look that went through her. "I did not consult you about the sleeping arrangement. I did not know if you preferred to be in his bed."

Blake looked a little shocked at the direction the conversation was not turning. How much is showing on her face? Was denial a clear admission of guilt? She was saying nothing or pausing too long, making her look like a fool. "I have never been in Spencer's bed." It was a clear statement that might move the conversation along or even allow it to change on its own.

"Since you got here, you have had a question on your face. You are wondering how it works since I am twenty years younger than my husband. You want to know because you want to know if the difference in your age and Spencer's would cause an issue."

"Look, we came here for something else. Something important."

"Love is important. And you love him. And since you did not ask, I will answer anyway. My life is wonderful. Buddy is the sweetest, kindest man I have ever met. I love him with all my heart. As for the age difference, it does not mean a thing.

Every minute I spend with him makes me feel warm and protected as for my giant family. It is unbelievable. I am a sister, mother, and even grandmother rolled into one. I never knew how much I hated the world out there until I came here."

Blake sat back on the old-fashioned bed. She felt she had been blessed with answers she would never have had the guts to search for.

Chapter 12: Welcome Home

"**M**an, am I glad to see you back?" Detective Walter Graves announced as Spencer and Blake entered the Tucker Street police station office. Spencer and Blake had dropped Morgan and TJ off at their hotel after the drive back from Winona. Spencer had dropped copies of the information provided for Detective Graves and his partner Kate Sharp to work on, allowing himself and Blake to rest late in their respective abodes. "When you are gone, everybody keeps asking me questions. The problem is they want Spencer answers. I can only give them Graves answers.

"I missed you guys too." Yolanda joined in. She was seated next to Detective Franklin, picking imaginary fleas off him. "I was going to start a rumor that the two of you were on your honeymoon, but you didn't give me quite enough time." She confessed eating some of the imaginary fleas.

"Newton from the DA's office and that Fed Reed keeps showing up trying to find out what we know."

Graves retrieved a piece of paper from a file. One of those sheets of paper from Buddy's ranch is a set of coordinates. There are two spots in Illinois, a little across the river. I am assuming we are going there. How do you want to do it?"

"Have Newton contact the DA's office in Illinois and get warrants for those locations." Spencer answered, then looked at Sharp find out who is Sheriff or who patrols that area and then wait until we are on our way and let them know we are coming to take a little look."

"How should I dress?" Yolanda asked.

"Everybody in body armor. If you got heavy weapons, feel free to bring them."

"You know, Spencer, I love having you home; otherwise, I have to take orders from our real bosses, and you know how much that sucks." Red confessed.

"One other thing, Spencer, Reed from FBI says if we roll out, she wants to come along."

"It's her ass."

"Tiny little thing that it be," Yolanda commented.

"I want to be on Highway 64 ten minutes after the paperwork is signed," Spencer announced.

"Who are we trying to get the jump on exactly?" Blake asked, confused.

"The press." The others sang out in unison.

Chapter 13 The Field of the Dead

S pencer could feel pangs of concern as the four unmarked police cruisers from the Major Case squad approached the Sheriff's office in Bowles County, Illinois. Bowles is a small township about three miles outside of Greenmount Crossing and even more unheard of by most. As the group approached, the first thing they noticed was that there was a news van in front of the Sheriff's office. It was clear that the Sheriff had invited them. Sheriff Chester Dodd, the Sheriff for Bowles, was a big man who looked like he may have been a professional wrestler in his early years but had allowed much of the mussel of his mass to be overcome with fat. His face still held to the cockiness of a man that wanted an opportunity to prove his male dominance even if male dominance was not the issue in question. His head had lost the battle with a come over and now stood in the recession of a war lost to time. The Major case team hurried past the newspersons and their camera people as quickly as possible, hoping to speak to Sheriff Dodd privately.

"Hells bells folks, we are all professionals here. The press has certain rights to collect a little information. Not that you will find much out there in the field where you are going. It may be possible that someone gave you bad information and look how convenient it will be to have the press here to set the record straight." Dodd stated from a squeaky, outdated office chair.

"Sir, any information you have released or plan to release may violate legal standards." Reed commented. She stood dressed like she was planning to invade a small nation and had been given the wrong sizes for all her gear.

"Ma'am, I don't know who you are trying to tell the law to, but this county is under my jurisdiction." Dodd proclaimed.

Spencer, Blake, and the rest of the Major case squad all smiled because they knew what was coming.

"Look, Homer...." She started.

"Chester." He corrected.

"Same fucking thing. I am with the Federal Bureau of Investigation. With the emphasis on Federal, so unless you are declaring this piece of shit dust bowl as a Sovern nation, you will yield to my authority, or I will have these lovely people who do happen to be working with me under the direction of the White House, lock your fat ass up." She gave him a stare that would melt granite.

A crestfallen look overtook the Sheriff's face, and without a word, he began leading them to his car to drive them to the area in question.

"I think it was the ma'am that did it," Yolanda whispered to Jackson.

"I don't know about you, but I am starting to like her," Jackson responded.

"Do they teach cussing at the FBI?" Blake whispered to Spencer.

"Only in the advanced classes."

THE GROUP WALKED CAREFULLY in a flat field. It was early fall, so there were colored leaves covering the ground? Blake noticed a small runoff from an underground spring or from excess irrigation. There as a pail red color to the leaves caused by runoff water.

"Damn." She yelled, and Spencer ran to her.

"Please tell me that is not what I think it is?" Graves questioned.

"What?" Reed asked, totally confused.

"What?" Sheriff Dodd could not wait for the answer.

"Everyone watch where you are stepping and back out just as you came in. Set up a police line and keep the press out of here at all costs." Spencer commenced.

"What is it, Detective?" Reed shouted into Blake's face.

"This whole area is a big graveyard. The graves are shallow and not in vaults like they do for funerals. We're walking on dead bodies." Blake answered.

Someone shrieked.

Chapter 14 GEAR CHECK

It did not take long before the entire area was shut down.

Uniformed officers with dogs and survey teams were marking areas. The Major Case Mobile Unit was brought out, and a great deal of on-site processing began.

Three hours into the process, the Major Case Detectives walked the area, giving uniformed officers and technicians instructions.

"I don't mean to be a bother about it, Spencer, but the first sheet of paper that led us here had coordinates for two locations, and this is only the first." Graves noted to Spencer once he was sure no one else was listening. "The second one should be down that path. Are you up for more of this shit, or do you want to wait?"

"No real choice, Walter. We have already started losing daylight, and I have seen what these people can do in the dark. Get my partner to lead us in; it seems field and stream is her forte."

"Alright, Major Case, we are on the move," Blake announced after a brief conference with Graves. "We will need a couple of uniformed officers who are not family-inclined to join us. Investigator Reed, you will be accompanying us as well."

She walked up to Reed, turned her around, and tightened up the strap holding her Kevlar vest.

"I can handle it myself." Reed proclaimed.

"No, you cannot. Spencer's rules when working with him are that each team member checks another team member's gear." She turned her back to Reed to allow her to check her harness.

"Good to go," Reed announced.

A high degree of pride swelled in Spencer. In Blake's short time with him, she never ceased to make him proud of her.

Chapter 15 THE HOUSES IN HELL

"You see that?"

Blake pointed to vines that were still growing even in late fall.

Spencer looked up. "Yes, I saw that."

"What is it?' Reed asked.

"It's a fishing line.

Someone strung it between the trees to encourage the vine to grow and create a natural cover. Drug dealers do this to block the site of their farms from the highway." Yolanda answered.

The group had been walking down the path, unsure where it led. They maintained quiet even though no one had requested it. The uniformed officers had silenced their radios. They could all sense that whatever was ahead of them was far worse than what they had just left. And what could be worse than an unmarked graveyard? The path led to a hidden clearing. In the clearing, there were five structures. One was a prominent garage. A main house sat in the center, and three large trailers separated from the main house. All the structures were old but maintained. It was clear someone had been there recently.

"Do you want us to knock?" Graves asked Spencer.

"Do it from the side and be sure." Yolanda covered him with the shotgun she was carrying.

Just as Graves went to knock on the door, a four-wheeler revved up and sprang from the bushes. A skinny man was driving the vehicle, and he had a Mack ten, and it was pointed toward Jackson, who was brought up the rear and thereby blocked the man's exit to the path. A loud boom rumbled, and seconds before the skinny man could shoot Jackson, Yolanda had pivoted and fired, blasting the man from the four-wheeler. The man landed in the dirt, but the bike kept moving, and Spencer grabbed Blake and pulled her just in time, not to be hit by the flying machine. They tangled in each other's legs, and both went down, with Spencer landing on top of Blake.

"Nobody shoots my monkey," Yolanda yelled.

It took a moment that seemed to last much longer for Spencer to get up and pull Blake to her feet. When they stood, they stared at each other for a moment in mutual embarrassment.

The uniformed officers rushed to zip-tie the skinny man, who did not seem hurt. The shotgun had hit his chest, and he also was wearing a protective plate.

"Going in." Graves yelled, kicking the door open. The inside of the house was horrific.

Someone had created a jail cell and torture chamber and surrounded it with the shell of a shack. There was dried blood and bones everywhere. There was the setup for waterboarding, shackles, and a chair for electric shock. In one of the cells that lit open, there was a corpse that was rotting.

Reed entered the room with the look associated with vomiting, and just before she could run from the stench and flies, something caught her eye in the cell where the corpse lay.

"No one touches anything; this has to be processed," Spencer stated more to Reed than his team. She bent down and reached into the mass of blood and remains and retrieved something.

"What is it?" Blake asked.

"It's an FBI shield. It's the same as mine. This poor bastard is one of ours."

The team investigated the property further. In the garage, they found the vehicles that had driven Spencer and Blake off the road, complete with the vehicle with the hole and shattered window.

There was a great deal of blood, in which no one could have survived the loss—and radio frequency jamming equipment.

In one of the tiny houses, they found the bodies of three women who were bound and shot in the back of the head.

"What do you make of this?" Spencer asked Blake.

"Test?"

"Yes, test."

"Some Central American Mercenary teams find prostitutes or kidnap young girls for sexual entertainment purposes. It keeps them from going into local pick-up places where they may be compromised.

When they are ready to move on, they eliminate those women because they may have heard things or transmit DNA that can lead to their capture." She answered.

"Holly shit, is she right?" Sheriff Dodd asked, looking at the girl's mangled lifeless bodies.

"Yeah, Homer, she's right," Yolanda answered.

"I recognize those girls from the truck weigh-in station on I-64. They spent a little time releasing the pressure for a few over-the-road truckers, but they didn't cause any trouble." He recalled.

"It's not your fault, Sheriff. It's all of ours for being a step behind these guys." Spencer muttered.

"You know who is responsible?" Blake asked as the entire group looked at Spencer.

"Knowing who is responsible for something and being able to arrest them for it are often miles apart."

Chapter 16 SO THEY CALL THE THING A RODEO

There had been two solid days of processing with these many active investigation scenes. Spencer and Blake stepped from the elevator, and Joy Alexander met them with an envelope. "Spencer, this is for you. I guess it's personal; that's why there is no return address. I didn't want to leave it on your desk because some of the jackals you work with can investigate the hell out of the wrong thing."

"Thank you." He accepted the envelope, looking forward at his desk, and noticed the IT department sitting in his seat texting.

"Detective Blake, do you mind if I have a moment alone with Spencer?"

Blake walked off as puzzled by Archie being seated at Spencer's desk as anything haven been said or asked. Yolanda sat at her desk staring at Archie, then surrounded him, thereby Archie was able to ignore her.

"Spencer, I don't know how to say this other than coming right out. So, I will. If you are dating again, I cook a really good meal. I know you have an aversion to policewomen, but remember, I am a civilian, and I can be discrete if you need to take things slow." Joy offered and waited for the acceptance of her offer.

"Joy, I will certainly keep that in mind. Right now, I need to pull these guys together as best I can."

She smiled as if she had made her point and was satisfied that the ball was now firmly in his court.

Spencer looked down at the letter. Having not recognized the handwriting, he opened the letter to check the sender as he walked to his desk.

"Who's the letter from?" Blake asked as he approached.

"Your mother."

Blake sprung from her seat, grabbed Spencer by the arm, and ushered him into a corner where she could discuss his last remark, or so she thought. Some of the others working in the room showed mild interest but lost interest as they disappeared from hearing range.

"Look, Spencer, there is no call to be rude. If it's about what happened the other day in that field by that house of death. I am sorry."

"Blake...." He tried to interrupt.

"Guys are always trying that on girls all the time, and I never had the slightest bit of sympathy for them. And there I go doing the same thing myself."

"Bonnie...."

"I mean if you hate me and would never accept my apology for feeling you up like that when you were only doing your duty." His face flushed. "I guess you could report me for sexual harassment or something."

He folded the letter and shoved it in his pocket. "Apology accepted; all is forgiven." He whispered. "Now, why don't we find out what brought Archie into the daylight."

"Can you guys introduce me to Maggie?" Archie asked, jumping from the chair as Spencer and Blake approached.

The second piece of paper given to Spencer by Uncle Buddy contained a list of names, followed by a row of numbers, then a code number, and a second set of numbers. Archie was now staring at his paper copy with some added notations.

"Maggie's not a real person," Blake informed him.

"You are the last person I would think would show prejudice," Archie exclaimed with his voice slightly raised.

"Hey, meathead, she is telling you Maggie is a computer," Yolanda yelled, having been interrupted by the paperwork on her desk.

"Then I guess you are just a lump of cells and protoplasm. She is not just a computer. A Commodore 64 is a computer. A Mack book pro is a computer. Maggie is a goddess, and it isn't out of line to ask for a little favor."

"They need to find a way to start pumping you guys some daylight or air or whatever it is that you guys need in the cave you call an IT department," Yolanda remarked, causing stares from all the workers, guests, and suspects that inhabited the office.

"What would someone like you know about evolutionary procreation?" Archie asked.

"Is he talking about having sex with a computer?" Blake asked, looking puzzled.

"Don't you understand she could be the next generation of Comstock?" He proclaimed.

"What the hell is a Comstock?" Detective Graves asked as he walked up to the exchange.

"It's my last name." Archie answered.

"He wants to fuck one of the computers." Yolanda simplified for Graves.

"That's pretty twisted even for IT guys." Graves remarked. "Surely he meant something else."

"On the subject of something else, Archie, other than entering your name into our computer dating service, for lack of a better expression. Did you have a hit on the info you were given?" Spencer asked, now desperate to redirect the conversation back to the case.

"Oh yeah, it's a moniker file," Archie explained.

"What is a moniker file." Detective Franklin asked to look up from his work.

"You see, any time a cop or fed goes undercover, not everything stops in his life that is a connection to their real name. For example, you still pay union dues; hopefully, you still get paid and pay taxes." Archie began.

"So, someone could, in theory, ask the computer or mainframe to find and match anomalies that meet the criteria of someone hiding his identity, even if that someone was an undercover cop?" Spencer confirmed.

"Yes, but you could not do it effectively with a standard computer.

They don't have the capacity and could not understand a set of command codes that vast. There is also a jungle of security obstacles, encryption too complexed for standard computers and hurdles blocking your way in or out. You would need a mainframe or mini mainframe that was not attached to the government computers directly."

"Why not directly attached to the Government's computers?" Graves asked.

"Because we are asking the computer to do something totally out of policy at the least and illegal at best. The government mainframe would know to report you to the correct people. Don't you guys see this is what makes her a Goddess?"

The group sat to process the information, and the lab tech in large glasses walked up and placed a file on Spencer's desk.

"Bigger problem, guys let's say we all go see Commander Davis with this one." He said, handing the report where they all could read.

Edmund Davis was having a discussion with a couple of uniformed officers. Still, when he saw the six detectives approaching his office, he rushed the officers out.

"I am supposed to be making my daily for the White House and the Governor. Of course, now it's Governor's plural since our little incursion into our neighboring state; they want to know what we are up to as well. That is why I am glad you guys came to my office. Because

I know with the pool of shit we seem to be swimming in, you have brought me a life preserver."

"Not even close boss." Spencer began. "There was a bullet in the head of that bloody mess in the cell of that Illinois torcher chamber. And we got a match."

"That fast?"

"It's local." Grave added, now handing the report to Davis.

"The gun was in the system because it belongs to a cop. Detective Ryan West. The ballistics are on record due to past shoot team reviews." Spencer added, looking at Davis, waiting for his next remark.

"Damn, looks like we got ourselves a Rodeo." Davis proclaimed.

The unit referred to the arrest and bring-in of an officer who is currently active as a rodeo.

"I'll call Newton with the DA's office and get your warrant," Davis stated.

Spencer turned to Detective Graves without saying a word. "I'll contact the officers' union and have a rep brought over in a blind alone with a public defender for technical purposes."

Spencer turned to Yolanda. "The guy's wife is a cop too. I will find out who her immediate supervisor is and have her taken off rotation in case we need her."

Spencer then turned to Jackson. "I will contact an assault team and have them ready to rock and roll. Let's get ahead of any possible standoff shit."

Spencer turned to Sharp, still not saying a word. "I'll find FBI Agent Reed; she was a little shaken up, but she deserves to be in on this."

Lastly, Spencer turned to Blake. "No rodeo would be complete without a couple of rodeo clowns. And I have just the two. Internal affairs guys I recently met who looked like they could stand some fun."

Spencer turned back to Davis. "Spencer, you train your people well."

Chapter 17 The Past Must Meet the Future

B lake stood in front of her open locker in the women's dressing room of the police station, getting ready to go and assist in serving the warrant and bringing in Detective Ryan West. She turned slightly and noticed she was being watched. Kate Sharp stood, waiting to get her attention. "I saw what you did to Spencer the other day when he fell on top of you."

Blake took a deep gasp. She was not sure of the level of humiliation she would endure.

"Can I call you Bonnie? It somehow seems to fit."

"Look, I don't know what came over me."

"You don't owe anyone an explanation. I may think I was the only one instead of Spencer who saw what you did, and it was because he was facing me. Oh, the shocked look on his face." Sharp stopped talking for a moment while two other women walked past them.

"Your secret is safe with me. I am not a gossip."

"You have no idea how much better that makes me feel."

"There is a favor I want to ask."

Blake was lost in the request. Was she in the clear or not, she wondered? Bonnie needed clarification on whether refusing the request, whatever it was, would cancel the silence agreement.

"There is someone who wants to meet you. She is an old friend of mine. And she would like a word or two." Sharp handed Blake a piece of paper with the name of a bar and the time 6:00 p.m. written on it.

"Is this something I should be keeping from Spencer? Your choice of meeting area tells me this is not the most public of conversations."

"I ask that you meet with her first. Then, if the two of you decide to talk to Spencer about your meeting, at least you will know what it's about." Sharp reasoned.

"Now, let's go find us a bad cop."

Chapter 18 THE ARREST

"You still have a fine ass, Yolanda." Detective West commented, and the arrest team entered his home. He had been in night court and was allowed to sleep in, so it was obvious that he had been waken.

"Show some respect for your wife, West, after today, she may be the last friend you have." Yolanda thew back. And he ignored it.

"You must be Spencer's new bitch." West addressed Blake in a gruff tone, clearly to rattle her.

"If I get the meaning correct, the answer is yes. Now these two guys are Internal Affairs Detectives Michaels and Sylvester; they are here to make you, my bitch." She responded.

Yolanda chucked at her spunk.

"So, bitch if you don't mind turning around so these real cops can hook you up, I will read you your rights."

"Hey, Spencer, what kind of crap is this. Everyone tells me how fair you are now you are letting this hillbilly girl scout push my husband around." Jada West came screaming from the bedroom. She had heard the exchange but chose to listen to specific parts.

"Officer, my people always stand their ground. You know that, and your husband damn sure knows it. He pressed the issue." Spencer commented and nodded for Blake to continue to read West his rights. Ryan West was a big man. He was larger than Spencer but not as large as Franklin.

"Old times, Franklin. Old times. Can't you see your way clear to throw a brother a bone?" West requested.

"Sorry, rap, the friendship train has left the station. It left the minute you shot a fed in the head. Somebody get his sorry ass out of here so we can take this place apart." Franklin responded angrily.

The internal affairs officers took West from the scene, and the rest of the team began searching the house. "I got the primary weapon on the list," Kate yelled, holding up a 9mm handgun.

"Keep going; remove any weapons from this address like it says in the court order," Reed ordered.

"I am a cop, too. You can't take my gun, you skinny-ass white girl." Jada roared. "And watch where you are throwing things; everything better be put back in place."

"Look, you idiot, I am taking all weapons, so I suggest you learn the alphabet and learn to file papers or learn to chalk tires or something. And no one here cares about your shitty decor. We will throw shit wherever we want. One more word out of you, and you will be seen as obstructing the execution of a lawful court order." Jada barely had time to make a retore before Reed snapped her fingers, and two uniformed officers handcuffed Jada and put her in the back of a police car for the duration of the search.

"Yeah, I think I am starting to like her," Yolanda commented to Jackson.

Chapter 17 A DRINK WITH THE EXPARTNER

B lake walked causally into the Fox Bar and Gril at exactly 6:00.
She could not remember being so nervous about meeting someone who should mean nothing to her. Seated at the bar, she saw a lady with her back to her.

The woman's suit was a tan with a perfect fit. She wore dark stockings and had a look of class that Blake could admire. The woman's hair and nails were perfectly done as Blake walked closer, observing the woman. "You must be Blake." The woman rose and extended her hand, aware of Blake's presence, even though Blake had no idea how the woman could have seen her approach. "May I call you Bonnie? A little birdy told me you prefer that when you are not working?"

Blake seated herself across from the woman, taking in the electric wave of her presence. "You can call me Lisa."

"I am not sure why I am here really," Blake confessed as a waiter walked to the table. "I will have a vodka martini, two olives, and one for my new friend."

"No. Not for me, club soda. I have to visit an 8-year-old girl to tuck her in later, and her mother has a drinking problem. I think it would be bad form to show up smelling like a still." Blake corrected. The waiter scurried away.

"Tell me Bonnie have you fucked him yet?" Lisa asked.

"Whoa," Blake screamed, jumping to her feet. "I think I made a mistake coming here." Before Blake could leave the table, Lisa grabbed her shoulders. "I'm sorry. Look, I am a cop. Sometimes we talk that way. I didn't mean to offend you if you could give me one last chance."

Blake reseated herself. "Look, I know you are one of his old partners—the last female partner before me. I just thought there were some, you know, tips you wanted to tell me about getting along with Spencer. I had no idea we were going to be discussing sexual histories."

"Fair enough. Then please allow me to lay my cards on the table.

First, I love Spencer. Tell me, does he still do that test thing that always has you ready to recite what is happening?"

Blake smiled a little, knowing Lisa knew Spencer's ways.

"Second, my love for him will always be in my heart."

The waiter brought the drinks, and Lisa took a long swig of the martini as if bracing herself for what she might say next.

"Next revelation. I am married."

"Does your husband know you are still in love with Spencer?"

Lisa smiled, reached her hand across the table, and patted Blake's hand. "Oh. I guess when people are saying bad things about you, sometimes you think it will never be over."

"I don't understand."

"I don't have a husband, my dear Blake; I have a wife. I am gay." Lisa stared directly into Blake's eye, giving her time for the comment to penetrate.

"I would have thought there were jokes or references to my lifestyle in the department by now. I married a woman from the St. Louis Fire Department over a year ago. We have been together for a long time, but we went through some rough patches."

Blake pulled her hand back. "Don't worry, it's not contagious, and I am not here on a drive." Lisa smiled.

"Why are we here?"

Lisa took another long drink. "Weren't you listening? Because I love Spencer, and I want to be sure he is taken care of. That no one hurts him." Lisa's eyes teared slightly. Blake knew she had to draw out of Lisa whatever was so important.

"Then take your time and tell me." Blake requested.

"Some time ago, we were partners and the closest of friends. He knew I was gay, but he did not care. He taught me and protected me, and somewhere along the line, I fell in love with him." Lisa began pausing to signal the waiter for another drink.

"You are a woman; he is a man; what's the problem?" Blake asked.

"Spoken like a true heterosexual. Our parts may match anatomically, but I could never give him the inner pleasure he needed and faking it would have been a total disaster for both of us. Also, keep in mind, he was married." The waiter arrived with fresh drinks. "At some points, rumors began about some of the male-female teams, and some of the woman confessed that they had slept with their partners. There was a joke going around that if you gave your partner a little pussy there was never any doubt that he would be there to watch your backside."

"I have heard that joke." Blake confessed, trying not to stop her from telling of the tale.

"When I heard the rumor, I, in a moment of trying to hide what I really am, perpetuated the rumor."

"You let people think the two of you were having sex when in fact, you were not?"

"I thought it was just a little white lie. Who could it hurt? After all, he was my best friend, and a friend helps you out sometimes, even if they don't know it."

"I take it this all fell apart."

"Like a watermelon in a cheap wet paper bag. His wife got the misinformation and began giving him shit. I could tell even though he assured her I was his friend and partner." She took another big drink. "Are you ready for the most fucked up part?" Bonnie nodded, staring at the woman who looked like a model when the story started deteriorating into a sad mess. "One day, we were set to go to trial on two cases—one in St. Louis and one in Chicago. Spencer knew I hated Chicago and offered to take the trip. He testified on the first day, and it was so clear and eloquent that the defense decided to take a plea. So, the weeklong trip that he planned only took a day. He got the night train out of Union Station and was back home that night. He went home and heard a noise coming from his bedroom. There was Tina, his wife, and mother of his children, having sex with a man Spencer thought was his friend." Blake looked in her drink, wishing it was stronger, then looked up at Lisa, and Lisa was in full tears.

"What happened? Did he divorce her?" Blake asked, unaware of anyone or anything else in the room.

"Oh, you poor girl, have they really kept you in the dark?"

"What, damn you?" Blake asked, pausing the next drink from going to Lisa's lips.

"Spencer took out his gun and beat the man within inches of his life. He put the gun in the man's mouth and was going to pull the trigger until Tina stopped him. The guy he beat is a cripple to this day. I think the best work he can find is a crossing guard somewhere." Blake sat back, looking like she had been through a marathon. "In for a penny, in for a pound, my dear," Lisa said, taking another drink and signaling the waiter again.

"What does that supposed to mean?" Blake asked.

"It means the story does not end there. Spencer refused to take Tina back after she saw the error of her ways. One day, Tina puts on her finest nightgown, writes a good-bye note to Spencer, and then blows her brains out. Now his two daughters won't ever speak to him."

"Oh my God."

"I help nurse Spencer back to health as far as I can tell, but if I thought for one moment you were out to hurt him, I would blow your brains out and take my chances," Lisa confessed.

Blake felt a warm moisture hit her hand. She did not notice that she, too, was crying.

"I promised my wife I would not be anywhere where Spencer is. You see, she is very jealous. But I have watched him from afar. He needs human love and touch, the kind I cannot provide. Now go and leave me here to pity myself for the spiral I put in motion that hurt the best person I have ever known."

Blake stopped at the bar and signaled for the bartender. She handed him a twenty, then flashed her badge.

"You see that woman over there.

You have over-severed her, and I am a cop. When she is ready to leave, you call her a cab, and she leaves alone. If I find out differently, you personally will be doing time.

Are we clear?" It was clear from Blake's tone it was not a question.

Chapter 19 HOW TO INTEROGATE THE INTERROGATOR

"Right this way." Detectives Graves and Sharp lead Major Bradley and Jackie. They were led into an interrogation room. The room was a small, closed with a one-way mirror in the wall.

There was a plain steel table in the middle of the room.

"Oh, damn looks like you got something on your uniform," Sharp stated to Bradley and began brushing something from the arm of his uniform. She took a moment and looked directly at him.

"Would you like water?"

Graves handed both of them small bottles of unopened water. "Spencer went to pick up some pictures he says he needs for the interrogation of Detective West."

"Did he say why he needs us?" Jackie asked, accepting one of the waters.

"No, Spencer is the big brain type. It can be hard to figure out what is on his mind, but he shouldn't be long. I am sorry about the accommodations, but this is a police station, and we have plenty of interrogation rooms." Graves smiled and left the room.

Graves and Sharp joined Spencer and Blake behind the one-way mirror.

"Okay, so you got to tell me how you knew." Graves requested.

"Then you might not read the book," Spencer answered.

Graves retrieved Bradly and Jackie in a few minutes and led them to the desk where Spencer and Blake sat with the rest of the team they had assembled.

"Would you like a donut?"

Blake offered to present a box of donuts and put it in front of Jackie. "Not for me. I am watching my weight." She answered.

"How about you, Major?"

"No, my wife says....."

Before he could complete his comment, Yolanda called out. "Busted."

"What is that supposed to mean?" Bradley asked.

"Simple, you two are acting like a couple hiding an affair. But you are not."

Jackie looked at the group and finally said. "It was me, wasn't it? No offense, but I don't do white guys. I guess I wasn't convincing. I like my men in a basic black." She stated then licked her finger and walked over to Jackson and wiped a little of the jelly overflow from the donut he had been eating from his face and stuck his finger in her mouth."

"No, it was the Major. No real dye in the Wool sleaze brags about his wife and praises his kids in front of his mistress. Also, when we saw you two at the hotel, he was late to pick up the flirt cue from you."

"Why are you letting that lady lick you," Yolanda asked, completely off-point to Jackson.

"So, you say I need better sleaze training. I will make a note. What else have you figured out?"

"Well, Jackie is an Army Officer, and so are you. You work for the DOD, but I would guess you are attached to the Department of Justice or, at the least, reporting to them. That would make you, her handler. How am I doing so far?"

"So, this is about blowing our cover?"

"No helping it." Spencer responded.

"You know, in my next life, I want to return as Spencer," Jackson remarked, and they all laughed.

"Well, before you go anywhere, be sure you make sure I get your number," Jackie stated, followed by a vicious stare from Yolanda.

Chapter 18 A Traitor's Walk

There was a deafening silence when the Internal Affairs offices brought Ryan West up to be interrogated. Every cop in the office stopped and stared at him. The worst thing cops can do is to be in a situation where they are charged with a major crime. Every interaction with past officers and suspects becomes circumspect. Since most police are honest and fair, they tend to resent anyone or anything that calls into question their credibility. But here it was, the storm that had arisen, and now there was nothing to do but head full speed into the mental darkness it conjured.

Detectives Graves and Sharp led Major Bradley and Jackie to the observation area where observers could view the integration without being in the room. Missouri DA Newton, Federal DA Huscamp and FBI Agent Shannon Reed joined them. The room was a tight fit, but no one complained. No one wanted to be the first to make the uncomfortable observation.

West was led into the interrogation room by two uniformed officers and chained to a metal table that sat in the middle of the room. Andy Ross, his legal counsel, joined him.

Ross was a small man who seemed to think wearing suits larger than his size made him appear larger; instead, he looked more like a small balding kid playing dress up. Internal Affairs Detectives Michaels and Sylvester took seats at the end of the table, and no one said a word as they all knew they were waiting for Spencer. The others were unsure if Spencer's late entrance was planned or if he had been collecting information that would prove germane to the exchange.

Spencer and Blake entered the interrogation room and stood behind West. Spencer was carrying a stack of what looked like pictures.

"Now that we are all here, let's get started," Michaels announced.

"I want to say for the record that my client is not going to have anything to say since no one here is offering anything," Ross spoke out.

"Counselor, we have 28 dead bodies from the gravesite. Another nine from the torture chamber. There are four from the house in Jennings and another six from the greatest highway fuck up of all time." Michaels began.

"Correction 5, and three-quarters from the highway. We are still picking up pieces when the wind settles down, and who knows what the number will look like in that graveyard if we ever stop finding bodies." Sylvester corrected, looking at Michaels for approval.

"I hear the EPA wants to fine you for how badly you screwed up the groundwater supply across the river." Michaels stopped and leaned forward. "Told them since you are looking at a death state-sponsored death sentence and a federal death sentence, our problem is how to execute you twice in two different places, so collecting a fine is chickenshit." Michaels laughed a hearty laugh.

West looked at his lawyer. "Don't get stressed. I used to do this myself all the time. Try to shock and scare the suspect into admitting something. It's a bluff, and the bigger the bluff, the bigger the offer, so they will come up with some spectacular offer." West informed his lawyer.

"Maybe we should keep our thoughts to ourselves, Mr. West."

"Hey, Spencer, I thought you and Honeybuns were running the show. Don't tell me after you left the job, you came back a pussy, and now you have these morons fighting your fight."

"Please be quiet, Mr. West; you are right. It is some game, but until we figure it out, it's we don't show or hand." Ross counseled.

Spencer walked around the table pulled up one of the remaining chairs and sat facing West and Ross. His back was to the internal affairs team. "He is right, Detective. I do not want you to say a thing." This brought raised eyebrows from the internal affairs team.

"What the hell is he doing?" Shannon Reed asked Graves and Sharp.

"Relax, it's Spencer, he's got him." Graves whispered.

Spencer removed a rubber band from the pictures and showed the first picture to West. The pictures had hand numbers on the back so Spencer could see West's face, and he looked at the pictures. West put a fake bored look on his face. Spencer placed the picture face down.

"What's this?" Ross asked.

"Just some pictures, Mr. Ross." Blake answered from behind West and Ross.

Slowly, one by one, Spencer held up the pictures. When the picture mark 22 on the back was shown to West, he flinched.

"Thank you, Detective West." Spencer stood and held the picture the against the one-way mirror so the people in the outer room could see it.

"That's a dirty trick Spencer," West yelled.

"What just happened?" Ross asked, totally confused.

"Let us in too Spencer," Michaels asked.

"It's called an autonomic recognition response. One of the pictures appeared twice. Detective West had to adjust to try and ignore it because he knew he had already tried to ignore the picture once." Spencer explained.

"No judge is going to for that. It sounds like a parlor game." Ross said.

Spencer smiled and looked at the mirror. "That wasn't for you. That was to have an arrest warrant placed on the person that set this all up. And since he is going to be charged with capital treason, do you think for one minute, he is going to risk his life over yours? The guy is going to be singing like the Temptations?" Spencer looked at Michaels and Sylvester, "We only need one body for the press, and former Detective West is volunteering."

"That's a dirty trick Spencer, that shit aint even in the books," West observed.

"Guess you just have to read my next book if it gets released in time. Have a nice walk back to your cell."

"Look, throw me a bone. I got things I can talk about here."

West began breaking down.

"Spencer, the man, is willing to deal. He had over 20 years on the force which should count for something. Don't be such a heartless bastard." Ross cried out.

"What could you possibly want, Judice?" Michaels asked.

"Nothing for me. It's too late. But my wife." West's tone had changed to a somber tone so different from the arrogance he had displayed at the start of the interrogation it was hardly recognizable. "I had three kids outside our marriage, and I even gave her the clap a couple of times, you know, night shift some hooker, what's to show her appreciation for letting her keep her stash or not locking up when we got her red-handed." West looked down sadder than ever. "She's too mean and too old to go back on the market. She doesn't deserve an asshole worse than me."

"Okay, let's say I have a question." Spencer led.

"Shoot."

"What did he recruit you to do?"

"I think you know. Interrogation. He had those animals for mercenaries, and they had no idea how to question people. They were slaughtering people, not even knowing when the person had given them all they had. The first night I was at the site, I said I would never return, but they kept throwing money at me."

"Tell me about the fed you shot in the head," Sylvester asked.

West stared down for a moment, and even Ross looked horrified.

"It was a mercy killing. They had broken the poor boy so badly. And they wouldn't stop. He looked at me and seemed to say with his eyes, if you have any soul left, put me out of my misery. I must have felt something, or I never would have used my service weapon. Maybe." And he left it at that.

Spencer stood up and walked to the door. "Hey, Spencer, the night you caught your friend laying the pipe to your wife. You know, if you had pulled the trigger, you would be on this side of the table. So why didn't you pull the trigger?"

Everyone in the room and behind the glass seemed to be waiting for an answer. "Because in a split second, I realized he didn't take anything she did not bring him there to get. So, if I shot him, I needed to shoot her too, and I couldn't do that. I could not shoot the mother of my children."

A wave of emotion swept over Blake, and she rushed from the room, went to her car, and cried. She now knew his heart. No matter how strong he is, he is unable to process betrayal completely. And he had be dealt a double dose of betrayal by the women closest to him.

Chapter 20 AND THEN THERE WAS THE LETTER

On a different level of the same parking structure, Spencer now sat in his car. He had left Michaels and Sylvester to their work. Spencer knew they would interrogate West with all the finesse of a pack of jackals attacking a baby zebra. There was no need for him to witness the carnage; he had cornered the poor animal and brought down its defenses. Spencer remembered the letter that Joy had and given him. He had been carrying it and now removed it from his pocket. He wondered where Blake went. He wondered what she thought of his revelation in the interrogation room. Most of all, he wondered why it meant so much to him.

And it did. He began to read.

My Dear Mister Spencer,

My name is Norma Butler Blake; I am Bonnie's mom. First of all, I hope you do not find it distasteful for me to be writing you, and we have never met or spoken. However, Bonnie has talked so much about you I feel you are like a friend of the family.

I want to thank you for the care and kindness you have been showing my daughter. I know she can be a bit wordy at times and a might exasperating with her singleness of focus, but from the sound of it, you have found ways to help her along. She has told me you are the best trainer and teacher anyone could ever have. She says they you are the smartest man she has ever known. There is one thing that concerns me, and I hope I am not overstepping my bounds since my daughter is 32 years old and a grown woman building her own life and experiences.

The best way to explain my concern is to tell you a little story about my girl. Back when she was breaking record and the University of Alabama, she was being sought for a place on the Olympic Track and Field team. She also had a female cousin who was also in contention. Her cousin was not and never be as good as my Bonnie.

Some people believe that Bonnie allowed her cousin to beat her on certain events to ensure the cousin would get into the Olympics. Her cousin did get in, but she bombed big time. The point is Bonnie never went to the Olympics even though she was the best qualified. She had placed friendship and family values above all the Gold in the world. I guess long-winded runs in the family, so I will just dive right into my concern. Every time my daughter mentions you lately, love bursts from seams. I don't even know if she is aware of where her heart has been led. I guess I am asking that if you do not or cannot share the same loving commitment to my daughter above being her mentor, for the love of God, find a good way to let her know.

Yours Respectfully,
Mrs. Norma Butler Blake

Chapter 21 THE SECOND MEETING THE SECOND TIME IS THE CHARM

"Let me thank you all for joining this meeting today and taking time out of your busy schedules for the matters at hand." Deputy Chief Edmund Davis began. The was pacing, circling the seated guest. The seated guest was Major Justin Bradley, DOD, Mr. Dorsey Homeland; Sanford Lowell, Attorney for Congresswoman Browser; Shannon Reed, FBI; Mr. Newton, Missouri DA; Mr. Huscamp, Federal DA, and Congresswoman Browser. The Congresswoman's aids trailed in and took seats.

Standing was Detectives Spencer, Blake, Sharp, Graves, Smith, and Franklin. Davis was what is referred to as a legacy cop. His father had been a cop, as had his grandfather. He had been taught that street cops think on their feet best, so he paced not restlessness but to keep the flow of his thoughts moving forward. "Joining us is Joy Anderson. She is here to record the information from today's meeting.

Also joining us via audio conference is Bolin Winters from the Justice Department and the White House Chief of Staff Jasper Watson." A brief noise that sounded like paper shuffling sounded on the conference phone that sat in the middle of the table. "This is Jasper Watson. I just want to say at this time, we have been joined by a high-level member of the White House staff, and for this call, he requests to remain anonymous."

There was a scratchiness on the conference, and Winters announced.

"I am not in the same location as Mr. Watson and his mystery guest, so at this time, I am asking that he verify for the record that his guest has proper security clearance."

There was a slight chuckling on the line, and Watson responded. "So, stipulated. He does indeed have clearance."

Davis was eager to get the meeting moving. "First, I would like to say that when this series of events began, I sat down with my Detectives one by one and asked if they had any problem working this case. To an individual that gave me a responding affirmation that they not only wished to be a part of this investigation but that they are Major Case, and this is what we do." He paused to look at his Detectives with pride. "I have presented to all of you a list of the events beginning with the assault on a Missouri County home and leading to the arrest of one of our own."

"Excuse me for interrupting Davis, but I hope you are not making deals and treating that rat bastard traitor with kid gloves." Winters spoke in a gruff tone. "I understand you guys are still pulling bodies out of a makeshift graveyard. When I heard there was a problem in St. Louis County, my mind raced back to those God-forsaken riots that sent a wave across the planet."

"Quite to the contrary, but we have other business now. And for that, I turn the meeting temporally over to the led Detective on the Case, Detective John Spencer."

"Mr. Dorsey, if you could stand up, please." Spencer requested and motioned to Detectives Sharp and Graves. Sharp and Graves began handcuffing Mr. Dorsey and reading him his rights."

"You can't do this. You assholes have no standing."

"Actually, they do. As per my contact with Ms. Reed, you have been a bad boy." Winters taunted. "What the hell were you thinking?

Moniker files to expose embedded agents. That sounds like the definition of treason to me."

Spencer nodded to Yolanda, and she and Franklin began handcuffing Donna and reading her rights."

"Look, you don't have shit on me. That drunken bitch is responsible." Donna screamed looking at Congresswoman Brower.

"I would have thought so too. That is why I was assigned to keep an eye on her. But when someone approved a military-style assault on her children, it caused me to rethink and recheck the facts." Jackie spoke up. "Whereas I do suggest you find a twelve-step program post haste, I doubt that you know enough about your own work to have pulled this off."

"Sounds like you guys have been busy trapping rats out your way." Watson remarked, and his guest laughed. "Just a second, my guest would like to say a word or two."

"Frequently, the events that make us most proud of who we are and what we are come from some of the most horrific circumstances. Today is no exception. My heart goes out to the Boone family. The family of a patriot who worked in the shadows to keep us all safe so that we might sleep soundly at night so often tend to go recognized. My heart goes out also to the people who were shoved into unmarked graves and to the families that may never have complete closure. Detectives and Staff, you will receive a letter accommodating you for your service in this matter. My greatest regret is that due to the nature of the beast, the letter may sound vague. But you know what you stand for and what you have accomplished." With those remarks, the group in Davis's office stared at each other. They knew it was the voice of the President of the United States.

SPENCER AND BLAKE SAT in the police cruiser outside the Department of Family Services. They had just appeared before a family court judge who wanted to hear all arguments that Amber Boone should be placed in the care of Morgan and TJ Boone. The judge has agreed with a couple of stipulations.

That all three undergo regular physical testing to determine the extent, if any, of their long-term health. And that Amber Boone is supervised at such time as the court sees fit. Morgan entered a request to take Amber to Winona, MS, for a service that is being conducted in honor of her father and for the wedding of Henry and Jennifer, two of their good friends. The judge agreed when Spencer and Blake offered to accompany them.

"I think we need to talk, Detective Spencer." Blake began.

Spencer sat staring out the front window, waiting. "I had a talk with your old partner. Now, don't be mad because it was not something I planned behind your back, but the details of how it came to be would violate another confidence."

"I see."

"See, I now understand about you and your wife." She stated, checking the look on his face. It had not changed. "I was not just the physical infidelity that hurt you. It was the emotional infidelity, And Lisa, in a way, committed the same type of crime."

"Blake." He tried to interrupt.

"No, just let me finish. I will never compromise our friendship.

I will never betray you. I understand emotional frailty. Now, is there anything you need to tell me?"

"Yes, the letter was from your mother. She wants to know if I am treating you well."

A look of shock overtook her face. "What did you tell her."

"Nothing yet. I haven't finished the letter I am writing in response."

"You aren't going to tell him I grabbed your thing, are you?"

"Have not decided." He smirked.

"Well, I could never go home."

"That would make the town population 27. What a shame."

"Will you do two things for me.?" She asked.

"Shoot."

"Sit down with Lisa and try to forgive her for the mistake she did."

"I will do that; what is the next?"

"Well, we are entering a new phase of our relationship. And since we are going to be going to Uncle Buddy's Farm. And since it is basically a baby-making farm, that is when they aren't testing weapons for the government or whoever. Let's start out on an even footing."

"What does that mean?"

"Well, if you just grab me here and give it a little squeeze."

"Blake."

"Yes." She murmured.

"You are right. I may consider calling you Bonnie at times like this.

Chapter 22 EPILOGUE

It did not take long after the second meeting to get the indictments rolling. Detective Ryan West was charged with 41 counts of accessory to murder under an open John Doe filing that would allow the Missouri District Attorney's office to fill in the names as the bodies were identified. He was also charged with one count of felony murder. Since the murdered man was an active Federal agent at the time of his demise, the Federal attorney's office also filed charges against him. He was charged with Espionage under the Espionage Act of 1917 and set for possible review for treason under 18 USC 2381.

Randel Dorsey was charged with 42 counts of murder and Espionage.

Investigation proved that Officer Jada West. Ryan West's wife had moved large sums of money into the accounts of her family members in an attempt to hide the inflow of cash from their ill-gotten gains. She protested, stating she was unaware of her husband's criminal activities. However, the moving of the money under the duty to act rule for law enforcement officers' states that if she is aware that a possible crime is being committed, she must respond. I short, if she did not know of her husband's criminal activities, she should have known. The act of hiding the money from Internal Revenue sources constitutes a crime, and such charges are being levied against both individuals.

Donna Bellflower was charged with Espionage, with evidence being collected for further charges.

Jorge Gutierrez, the ground keeper who was discovered at the killing shack, was first charged with seven counts of attempted murder. However, it was discovered that Mr. Gutierrez is illegally in the United States. When the member of the Mexican State Department realized he had been arrested, they requested he be sent back to Mexico for arrest and to answer questions.

They were so excited to find out he was apprehended they offered three US prisoners in exchange for his return. The US State Department agreed to take Americans currently serving time in Mexican jails. The US State Department is said to be holding an internal lottery to determine which US Citizens will be returned to the US since Mexico gave the 26 possible cases to choose from. The US State Department is also considering adjusting the time for the returned prisoners due to the fact that the segregation of serious offenders and minor offenders is not the same priority as Mexican Prisons. Also, an adjustment for being imprisoned so far from home was mentioned as an unnecessary hardship imposed. The US news sources got news of this impending trade and started referring to it as the Mexican buy one get two free sale. Most politically minded persons are waiting to see the general response from the public before weighing in on the possible arrangement.

After a meeting with the President of the United States and the head of her party, Congresswoman Browser announced she would not be seeking reelection. She cited medical reasons and a need to focus on family.

After more than two weeks of indictments and altering charges against government agency members, the President of the United States issued a formal statement. He stated that his administration was in no way asleep at the wheel and would not now or in the future tolerate a hot or cold war between government agencies. He further stated that he would comprise a committee to investigate transgressions that hindered the efficiency of one agency for the betterment of another. Much of the press thought the message was a case of the President attempting to make his job and involvement seem more critical and challenging than that of other presidents, therefore patting himself on the back. The persons at the focus of the message understood what was being said and why. If they persist, they were invited to do so at their own risk, and the risk would outweigh any possible reward.

Also by Alex Mitchell

Welcome to Shepherds Pass
Revenge at Shepherds Pass
Treasure at Shepherds Pass
Welcome to Shepherds Pass
Man Among the Missing
Noreen Tyler
Robinhood at Shepherds Pass
That Which Makes Us Who We Are
Secrets That Bind Family
Balance of Power in Shepherds Pass
All Gods Children
The Mole Hunters Children